GO AWAY DEATH

THE DEPARTMENT Z SERIES

GO AWAY DEATH

DEPARTMENT Z

JOHN CREASEY

OPEN ROAD

INTEGRATED MEDIA

NEW YORK

Copyright © 1941 by John Creasey

ISBN: 978-1-5040-9215-9

This edition published in 2024 by Open Road Integrated Media, Inc.
180 Maiden Lane
New York, NY 10038
www.openroadmedia.com

GO AWAY DEATH

1

LOFTUS IS DELIGHTED

S tanding by the window of his Brook Street flat, with a cigarette in one hand and a tankard of beer in another, William Loftus looked with interest at a telegraph boy cycling erratically along the road.

Loftus was a large man, by no means handsome, but with a face which, when he smiled, could be extremely attractive. He had a full, sensitive mouth. His eyes, one a shade higher than the other, often narrowed as if with weariness; they did then.

'Your trouble, Ned,' he said, looking away from the window, 'is congenital laziness allied to incurable romanticism.'

Ned Oundle, sprawled full length on a settee, regarded him without reproach. He was painfully thin, so that his features at times looked gaunt, but they were relieved by his enormous eyes, round as with innocence, fringed with most unmasculine lashes.

'What you mean is that I'm in love but too lazy to do anything about it,' he said mildly.

'A man in love is never too lazy to do anything about it,' said Loftus. 'Whoever the girl is—'

A ring at the front-door bell interrupted him.

Oundle closed his eyes, and heard Loftus say:

'Well, young man?'

'Cable-fer-yer-sir,' said a piping voice.

Oundle heard the tearing of an envelope, then a sharp exclamation which made him open his eyes abruptly. The possibility that there was bad news faded immediately, for Loftus uttered a sound that was very nearly a whoop, and said heartily:

'Sonny, you are a bearer of good tidings! Here's half-a-crown. No, no reply.'

The door closed on the boy's startled 'ta!' and Oundle uncoiled himself from the settee, saying severely:

'Why the unseemly generosity? What—'

Loftus smiled happily. 'Di's coming over.'

'Did she say what's bringing her?'

'No. Here's the cable.'

Oundle glanced at it, finding only a brief statement that Diana Woodward was leaving New York that morning, hoping to be at London Airport about three o'clock.

There had been a time when Oundle had resented Diana, for until her appearance on the scene Loftus had shown no serious interest in women, and had been well satisfied to work in his peculiar way, with Oundle as his often-present companion. A friendship of twenty years, thought Oundle, had been on the point of being broken, or at least damaged.

But Oundle had reckoned without the requirements of Department Z—a department once held up to ridicule by the Press, and by others who turned up their noses at the thought of an ultra-secret service. The activities of the Department, however, had become so widespread and had so often hit the front pages of the national papers that now the scoffing was heard only in odd corners, and about Loftus and other members of Department Z there had sprung a legend.

Loftus at that time was the leading agent in Department Z, which did not mean that he was its leader. That onerous, often thankless task was Gordon Craigie's; but Loftus was the man of action, while Craigie held the strings, sitting in his large office in Whitehall and sifting the enormous multitude of reports from sources as far afield as China and the Far East, Lapland and Greenland.

About the time that Bill Loftus was driving into London Airport to fetch Diana, Gordon Craigie was examining some reports which lay on a large, light-oak desk. It had several telephones, some manilla folders, and a blotting-pad, but nothing else except the papers Craigie was reading. He was wearing horn-rimmed spectacles, a recent innovation, and one to which he was not yet fully accustomed; long, white fingers fiddled with the spectacles as he read.

He was a man of medium height, thin, and lantern-jawed. His hair was grey, a small bald patch showing at the crown.

He looked up suddenly.

A faint click sounded in the otherwise silent office, large and, at one end, furnished with only the bare necessities of desk, filing cabinets and, by his side, a dictaphone. By the mantelpiece at the far end were several easy chairs, a small table, a bookcase and a cupboard, the door of which gaped open to reveal an astonishing miscellany of articles. A collar poked from one shelf; a jar of jam, half-empty, showed on another.

A green light was shining on the mantel-shelf.

Craigie pushed his chair back, approached the far end of

the room, and pressed a button beneath the shelf, close to the green light. A faint whirring sound was followed by the opening of a sliding door, and into the room stepped the most-photographed figure in Great Britain.

On a square, rather pale face, the sensitive lips were twisted in an ironic smile. Wide-set eyes of intense blue looked at Craigie with the same amusement. Dark clothes covered a figure which would have been tall but for the hunched, rounded shoulders, shoulders befitting a young bull. The short neck increased the bull-like impression, as did the quick but sturdy movement of the man, none other than the Prime Minister, the Rt. Hon. Graham Hershall.

Craigie pressed the button again, and the door closed behind his visitor, who pulled a flat silver case from his pocket and stuck a thin, dark cheroot into the corner of his mouth.

'Why the deuce do you go in for these melodramatic trimmings, Craigie? Well, what d'you want to see me about?' He sat down.

Craigie said slowly: 'American co-operation, sir. There is a growing movement in the States which believes that all we're trying to do is to make sure America pays the cost of English defence. In the last two or three days, prominent industrialists who in the past have supported generous contributions to N.A.T.O., and the acceptance of British membership, are veering round. They're big corporation men, they're making good and reasonable profits out of supplying N.A.T.O. countries with arms, but they're changing their attitude without any apparent reason. There must be a reason.'

Hershall pursed his lips.

'Ye-es. How many are involved?'

'Five, to date,' said Craigie. 'And Washington is worried by it. One man, Cyrus K. Hoppermann, is flying from New York to England this morning. I expect he's landed by now. Washington has sent an agent after him, and asked me to contact that agent, and to watch Hoppermann. He's probably the most influential of those who have changed sides recently.

Hershall was frowning.

'Hoppermann, Hoppermann. President of the Nu-Steel Corporation. I hardly expected him to change his mind.'

'No one did,' said Craigie dryly, 'but he has. He gave a television talk two nights ago, saying that he had information suggesting that America was being cheated, and that he was coming to England to see for himself.'

'Fair enough,' said Hershall.

'Ye-es. But will he be fair—and even if he is, will he be allowed to remain so? So far,' added Craigie, 'there isn't anything more to work on than the unusual *volte face* of Hoppermann and others, and Washington's anxiety about it. But I've information from other sources over there. The men who have suddenly changed have, with the exception of Hoppermann, altered in other ways. One has been seriously ill. Another has hired four men as a bodyguard, will only sleep with two of them in his room, and is obviously frightened out of his wits—*but neither has applied for Federal help.* What's getting at these men? Why are they afraid?'

Hershall sat back, eyes narrowed, smoke curling slowly from his cheroot. He said nothing.

'I can't answer any of these questions,' Craigie went on, 'but Hoppermann's arrival in England, and the purpose of his visit, might give us an idea. I propose to have Loftus and the others working on him immediately, and I think you should know that I feel it essential that they get results, whatever the difficulties of the job. Hoppermann would not be inconvenienced in any way that would give him cause for complaint, of course.'

Hershall widened his eyes.

'What's that? *Your* men work without giving cause for complaint? Don't try to blarney me, Craigie, whatever else you do! Loftus will do exactly what he thinks should be done, and damn diplomacy. H'm. You've nothing else?'

'Not yet.'

'All right.' Hershall stood up, speaking crisply. 'If you do anything to make a fool of me, or to jeopardise our relations, I'll give up trying to rely on any of these pesty departments.' He smiled suddenly. 'No offence, and don't take any.'

After he had gone, Craigie sat silently in his chair for some seconds, shrugged, then picked up one of the telephones. After a short delay, he was speaking to Ned Oundle.

'Craigie,' said Craigie. 'E-I-G—'

'Go on,' said Oundle, who had in any case recognised his chief's voice, but waited to hear the name spelt backwards; by such a simple trick it was possible for all Department Z agents to make sure that telephone calls were genuine; the simplicity of the system probably explained its effectiveness, for no one had ever misused it.

'Where's Loftus?' asked Craigie.

'Didn't you know? Diana's flying in from New York this afternoon, and he's gone to fetch her from the airport. But he'll be back any minute—her plane was due in at three o'clock.'

'Three o'clock,' echoed Craigie. 'That's the 'plane Hoppermann took; an American V.I.P. we're anxious to have a word with. So Diana actually travelled with him? I'll be over in half an hour or so.' He hung up without saying goodbye.

At the other end of the line, Oundle heard the click of the replaced receiver, and he too hung up. A moment later he heard the front door open, but no sound of voices. Loftus came in, alone, his face set.

Oundle waited, and Loftus said at last:

'Diana didn't get here. Nor did the 'plane. It exploded in mid-air—no one was saved. No one,' he repeated slowly, and in his eyes there was a pain which Oundle hated to see.

2

NO SURVIVORS?

After a pause, Oundle held out his cigarettes, and Loftus took one and lit it mechanically, flicking the match into the fireplace.

Oundle found words difficult to utter.

'How did it happen?'

'No-one knows,' said Loftus harshly, 'but it looks like deliberate sabotage.'

Oundle frowned. 'This might be something to do with Hoppermann.'

'Who's Hoppermann?'

'An American big-shot who was travelling in the same 'plane—'

He went no further, for there was a ring at the front door, and Craigie was admitted. He must have heard what had happened for he stepped towards Loftus, and placed a hand on his shoulder.

'I would rather anything than this, Bill.'

Loftus managed a ghost of a smile—bleak, unnatural.

'Well, we can't undo it. You lost your man, didn't you?'

'Ned's been talking, I can see,' said Craigie. 'Yes, Hopper-mann was on board, and it wouldn't surprise me to know that it was brought down to make sure he was killed. And,' Craigie went on slowly, 'he was coming to England to ascertain certain facts for himself, about—'

He talked for ten minutes, going through most of what he had already said to Hershall. He knew that Loftus was hardly listening to him; Loftus was seeing Diana, who had been coming to visit him for the first time in two years.

There was only one thing that would help him.

A period of inactivity would be disastrous, Craigie knew; but one of urgent action, such as appeared to be brewing, would ease his tension and, would help make the shadows recede. As he finished, he said quietly:

'Washington told me they were sending someone over with Hoppermann, Bill. It would probably be Diana.'

'Yes,' said Loftus bitterly. 'Damn them, why didn't they let her stay there? And what are we going to do about it? Isn't there any angle in this country at all?'

'Not yet.'

'I suppose we're looking for one?'

'Everywhere,' said Craigie, rather relieved by Loftus's abrupt manner. 'There's a Hoppermann office in London, of course, and I'm having it watched. We may get a lead from that.'

Loftus looked at him narrow-eyed.

'Who's watching?'

'The Errols.'

'I think I'll see them,' said Loftus. He stepped towards the door, then half-turned. 'Sorry, Gordon. I needn't tell you that I'm only half answerable for my actions. You've no reason why I shouldn't try the Hoppermann London office, have you?'

'None at all,' said Craigie, 'we need a line on this side badly,

Bill. But take this before you go.' He took a photograph of Hoppermann from his breast pocket.

'If there's a clue at that office we'll find it,' said Bill Loftus, taking the photograph. In a few seconds he was out of the flat and hurrying down the stairs.

Except for a certain oddness in voice and manner, the Errols did not notice any difference in Loftus.

They were cousins, both tall and good-looking, and possessing a remarkable likeness which often caused them to be mistaken for twins. Michael Errol was fair-haired, had a high forehead, a straight nose, full and well-shaped lips and a massive chin. Mark Errol was not quite so fair, and his hair was never so well-groomed as his cousin's. That, even to those who knew them well, was the main difference between them.

Loftus found Mike walking outside a large office building in the Strand. Mike was smoking, and he looked bored, but his eyes widened at the sight of Loftus.

'Hallo,' he said. 'What's brought you along?'

'Anything to report?' asked Loftus briefly.

'I don't think so,' said Mike. 'A lot of people have gone in, and a lot have come out. Mark's inveigled himself into the good graces of a girl in an office on the same floor as Hoppermann's suite, and he's alternatively making eyes at her and watching the passage. He'll have a better idea of who's gone in and out than I have.'

'Good,' said Loftus, and he walked into the building, while Mike looked after him in some surprise. Then he assumed that the case was more important than events had so far made likely, and prepared for sudden action. Loftus and action had a surprising habit of going together.

Loftus, finding that Hoppermann's office was on the second floor, ignored the lift and walked up. There was only one other firm on the second floor landing, and the door of its general office was standing open. The door was marked in black:

Leathercraft Journal
A. J. Makin, Editor and Manager.

Suddenly the door swung open, and Mark Errol appeared. He turned to say something to a girl whom Loftus glimpsed behind a counter piled up with, presumably, copies of *Leathercraft*, then closed the door and walked towards Loftus.

'I've been wondering how long it would be before you got here.'

'Well, I'm here now,' said Loftus shortly. 'Anything out of the ordinary happened?'

'He's arrived,' said Mark.

'What was that?'

'He's arrived,' repeated Mark. 'The big-shot. He's been here about an hour.'

Loftus took the photograph of Hoppermann from his pocket.

'Do you mean this fellow?'

'Of course I do,' said Mark. 'Aren't I waiting to see him, and to follow him when he comes out?'

'Ye-es,' said Loftus, and he brushed a hand across his forehead. 'Yes, of course. Stay here, and don't be surprised at ructions.'

He went past Mark, towards a glass-panelled door on which was printed:

Hoppermann's Inc.

He did not trouble to knock, but opened the door and stepped into a large, airy and well-furnished office. A staff of five or six women were sitting at desks or typewriters. No one looked up as he entered, although from one corner a diminutive boy with a mop of ginger hair approached without diffidence.

'Yessir?'

'I want to see Mr. Hoppermann,' said Loftus.

'Only by appointment, sir.'

'I see,' said Loftus. 'Which is his room?'

'He's in Mr. Sell's room, sir.' The boy eyed Loftus steadily, and even straightened his shoulders, as if to offer resistance should the visitor attempt to defy him.

'It's most urgent, sonny. Will you take a message?'

'Mussent,' said the boy promptly. 'Got orders.'

Loftus turned as if to leave, then suddenly swung round and strode towards a door on the left hand side of the office marked 'A. J. Sell.' The boy gasped, in ineffectual astonishment.

Loftus turned the handle, and the door opened.

He had a vague impression of a short, thick-set man smoking a cigar, a tall, lean, willowy man standing by a desk, and an equally tall but much heavier-looking man whose back was turned towards a window overlooking the Strand.

It was on this man that Loftus's eyes focussed.

He was middle-aged, his thick hair heavily streaked with grey, lending a distinguished touch to an already distinguished appearance. A fresh, healthy-looking face, a pair of blue eyes just then very frosty, a long nose with a high bridge, a square jaw. Loftus recognised him immediately; the photograph in his pocket was an excellent one.

The lean, willowy man spoke.

'Kindly go, *at once*, whoever you are.'

Loftus smiled, then addressed Hoppermann. 'You are Mr. Hoppermann?'

'I have nothing to say to the Press,' said Hoppermann coldly.

'You're going to be surprised,' said Loftus. '*I* have news for *you;* I am not asking for a statement. You're dead. You died when your aeroplane crashed. Didn't you know?'

3

DANGER FOR HOPPERMANN

It was a trick, and a well-tried one. Loftus had rarely known it fail him, and it did not then. Prejudice against him, refusal to receive him, faded away because of the sensation he caused.

'It's true,' he continued mildly. 'I have it on the highest authority. Are you yourself, or a good imitation? How did you get to England, Mr. Hoppermann?'

He acknowledged the American's ability to take a jolt and recover quickly, for Hoppermann's tension eased, and he drew away from the window.

'Who are you, sir?'

Loftus took a card from his wallet.

It was one of several he carried with him, and it declared him to be an agent of the Special Branch of Scotland Yard, instructing all officers of the Yard and constabularies throughout the country to afford him all possible assistance. He used it when he felt the need for authority and did not want to mention Department Z.

Hoppermann frowned down at it.

'A representative from Scotland Yard, Mr. Loftus?'

'That's so,' said Loftus slowly. He had garnered the fruits of the surprise attack, and the others had now had full opportunity to recover their poise. He saw no purpose in withholding anything else. When he had finished the outline of the story, there was not the slightest doubt that Hoppermann was nervous, although he made a commendable effort to hide it.

'This is extremely worrying, Mr.—Mr. Loftus.'

'If I read this affair rightly,' said Loftus, 'a murderous attack was made on a man believed to be you—always assuming, of course, that you're not an imposter.'

Hoppermann waved a hand at the willowy man, who appeared anxious to speak.

'Be quiet, Sell. That—er, that is an understandable suggestion, Mr. Loftus, but my staff here and many friends and acquaintances can vouch for me. And the Embassy, of course. You will have guessed what happened?'

'I think so.'

'Why don't you let him give his guess?' demanded the thick-set man sharply.

'That suits me,' said Loftus, 'You came over by one aeroplane but allowed it to be thought you were travelling in another. That suggests you knew there was some degree of danger.'

Hoppermann said slowly: 'Danger? Perhaps so. I was more anxious to avoid publicity on my arrival in this country, Mr. Loftus, and employed a man to make the journey by air. I left America by ship, and we berthed early this morning.'

'There was a television talk,' said Loftus.

'I recorded it before I left.'

'And the other man was so like you that he could take your place with impunity?'

'Hardly with—'

'Why don't we stop this yapping?' demanded the thick-set man. 'We don't even know the guy's a policeman. He could be a news-hound giving you a run round.' He was glaring at Loftus as he spoke, and his deep-set eyes did not look friendly.

'Why don't you telephone Scotland Yard?' asked Loftus. 'Superintendent Miller or Sir William Fellowes will satisfy you.' He turned away from the man, and addressed Hoppermann. 'If you didn't know there was danger before, you do now.'

'Aw, quit talking.' The thick-set man was irrepressible. 'What danger? Other airplanes have crashed, haven't they? And other guys have died.'

'I'm beginning to dislike you,' Loftus said softly. 'Supposing you keep quiet?'

'I am not impressed by your manner,' Hoppermann put in.

Loftus raised one eyebrow.

'No-o. You wouldn't be. I'll explain it, and it will give you an idea why I mean to see this through however it ends. Your— stooge was followed from America by a woman agent detailed to see you safely to England. She was in the 'plane. She was my *fiancée*. I have no peculiar and perverted ideas about your indirect responsibility for her death, but I propose to find who killed her.'

'The ruddy Commies,' broke in the thick-set man.

Hopperman froze him.

'If you can't keep silent, Goss, you can get out.' There was a pause, while Goss muttered something under his breath. Then Hoppermann went on: 'I won't say I'm sorry, Mr. Loftus, you won't want words. Obviously you doubt the direct responsibility of the Communists.'

'At the moment I doubt everything,' said Loftus. 'I start from one apparently unassailable fact, that someone meant to prevent you getting to England.'

'It could be so,' said Hoppermann; he had lost a little of his colour.

Goss said sharply: 'It could have been someone else they were after. Who else was on the 'plane?'

'No one of outstanding importance,' said Loftus.

'I told you to keep quiet, Goss.' Hoppermann gave the impression that unless he was obeyed Goss would get marching orders. 'I've assumed, Mr. Loftus, that you're satisfied that the 'plane was sabotaged to kill me? What else do you think?'

Loftus shrugged. 'I hardly need to say it, do I? If you were in danger then, you're in danger now. Once it becomes known you weren't on that aeroplane—' He paused.

Goss burst out: 'It's one of these smooth British tricks to stop you getting around. They want to put you away somewhere safe, where you can't see what's what.'

Loftus ignored him. 'Mr. Hoppermann, in my opinion you are in constant danger of your life. Your murder in this country would do an enormous amount of damage to Anglo-American friendship. If I were you I would go to the American Embassy without losing time, and—'

He stopped abruptly.

There was a bang somewhere outside, followed by a shout, and a scream from one of the girls, a hurried footstep and, from somewhere further off, Mark Errol's voice pitched on a high note.

'Watch it, Bill, watch it!'

Then the door burst open.

A little man, wild-eyed, dressed in poor, almost ragged clothes, stood for a moment on the threshold. Behind him was the red-haired office boy, the strained faces of the girls, and, by the outer door, Mark Errol.

Loftus moved towards Hoppermann, covering him.

The little man had one hand in his pocket, and snatched it out, shouting:

"Oppermann, you ruddy Yank, you ain't fit to lick an Englishman's shoes, you—'

Loftus saw the object in his hand; it was not unlike a hand grenade. The little man lobbed it towards Hoppermann, and it looked as if it would pass over Loftus's head. Loftus stretched up his arms, much as he would move towards a high catch in the slips, touched but could not hold it. He moved his hand backwards, touched it again, and sent it upwards, away from Hoppermann and through the open window. It fell from sight; and after what seemed an interminable time, there came a loud explosion.

After the explosion there was a moment of silence which seemed absolute. Then the little man moved, ducking to get past Mark Errol, but was too slow. Mark's hand shot out, and gripped his collar. The man turned and kicked at Mark's shin, landing one kick which made Mark gasp, but did not make him release his hold.

The man was screaming: 'Ruddy Yank, who wants the ruddy Yanks? They ain't got no guts, ain't got no—'

Loftus reached him, jerked him round with his left hand, sending in a right-arm jab. The blow was so well-judged that it clipped the man's teeth together, jolting his head back, and he slumped down on the floor, escaping Mark's grip only when he was in no state to get away. Again there was a moment of silence, then a typist began to utter a series of earpiercing shrieks which echoed through the offices.

The red-haired office boy moved quickly to a desk, picked up a water-jug, filled a glass, and calmly threw the contents into the typist's face. She gulped, gasped, and collapsed into an incoherent muttering.

Loftus turned to Mark.

'Stay there, will you? And send the youngster down for Mike.' He pulled the would-be assassin across the threshold and into the inner office, shutting the door behind him, and regarded the three men expressionlessly.

Goss was scowling.

Sell was smoothing his dark hair with an unsteady hand.

Hoppermann looked at Loftus.

'You—you were right, I guess. I'll do whatever you suggest.'

'That's fine.' said Loftus. 'The little fellow served a purpose after all. He must have convinced even Goss, and that couldn't be called easy.'

'I'll handle Goss,' said Hoppermann. 'After all he is my—' He hesitated for a moment, concluding lamely '—private secretary.'

The remark puzzled Loftus, but he pushed it to the back of his mind.

'Goss certainly needs handling,' he said. 'Are you taking him to the Embassy with you?'

'Yes,' said Hoppermann decisively.

'No,' said Goss with equal decision, and much more loudly. 'This guy might scare you off, Boss, but he don't scare me, not by a long way. I'm taking a look-around.'

Loftus smiled. 'Mr. Hoppermann is important,' he said. 'I can't imagine you being important enough for anyone to want to kill.' He did not wait to see Goss's reaction to his words, but stepped to the door. When he opened it both the Errols were outside, the gingerhaired lad between them, his chest puffed out, his eyes shining with excitement.

Loftus waved a hand towards the two cousins. 'One of you will take this customer'—he indicated the assassin—'to Cannon Row, and hold him under a charge of attempted murder. The other will follow Mr. Hoppermann and me to the

American Embassy. Have the regular police been making enquiries about the explosion, by the way?'

'Yes,' said Mark.

'We satisfied them that we knew what we were about,' said Mike. 'The only damage was a few broken windows and some palpitations.'

'Good. I think that we can go now.'

Then the little man moved again.

The odds were heavily against him, but he tried, showing no disinclination to fight. Diving across the floor, he passed and kicked at Mike Errol's knees, making him stagger. He was within Mark's reach, but Loftus moved with the surprising speed of which he was capable on occasion, and lunged against Mark, preventing him from catching the little man. At the same time he muttered into Mark's ear:

'Follow him.'

The girls were staring in dumb stupefaction at the wild-eyed man who was making for the door, all unaware that Loftus had deliberately let him go.

The ginger-haired office boy was also unaware of this.

The boy's lips pursed suddenly, and his eyes narrowed. He twisted round swiftly and made a flying jump for the little man, landing short and going flat on his stomach with a crash which shook the room, but appeared to leave him unaffected. The assassin had a hand on the door-knob when the boy's outstretched fingers gripped his ankles. The little man lost his balance and fell heavily, striking his head against the parquet floor; he would be out of action for some minutes.

The boy clambered to his feet, beaming at Loftus.

'Okay?' he demanded, triumphantly.

'If you—' began Mark sharply.

'Hush!' said Loftus, and then gravely. 'Okay, sonny. You did a good job that time. All right, Mike, take the little customer along.' He was close to Mike, who had recovered from the kick at his knees, and added in a voice none of the others could hear: 'Let him go. Keep after him.'

Hoppermann turned to Loftus and said with a peculiar little smile:

'Shouldn't we be going?'

'We certainly should,' said Loftus.

'If you ask me, you're plumb crazy!' grated Goss.

Then came a sensation, mild in degree but almost as startling in fact as the attempted murder. Hoppermann took two long strides across the office and with the flat of his hand slapped Goss's face so hard that the man reeled against the desk and then fell to one knee.

4

MIKE TAKES A RUN

The slap resounded through the office, and Goss stared up at Hoppermann with an expression of such fury that it would not have been surprising had he flown at his employer. He muttered something under his breath, straightened up and rubbed his cheek, which showed a red glow from Hoppermann's fingers, then lit a cigarette with a trembling hand.

Hoppermann looked at Loftus apologetically.

'I guess it's the only way to make him obedient,' he said. 'Goss is strongly convinced that the British are cheating us, Mr. Loftus.'

Loftus shrugged. 'Supposing we forget it? Is there anything you need to say to these people?'

'They can come to the Embassy to see me, later,' said Hoppermann. 'I'd like to get along.'

It was all too obvious that he was feeling very nervous, and there was nothing to occasion surprise in that. Loftus nodded to Sell and Goss, and went out of the office. Mark followed him, with Hoppermann. Mike was sitting on a chair and regarding the little man, who this time was coming round with genuine bemusement, blinking in the light from the window.

Hoppermann's arrival at the Embassy caused some consternation. This was not surprising since his death had already been announced.

Loftus explained, then left Hoppermann at the Embassy, and decided to walk to Craigie's office. As he went, a tall, lanky man followed him; following the lanky man was Mark Errol.

Mike Errol, meanwhile, had left Hoppermann's office with a hand on the wrist of the would-be assassin, who appeared to be still suffering from the effect of his second knock-out. Twice, however, Mike caught a quick, crafty glimpse from little beady eyes, and like Loftus he came to the conclusion that the prisoner was an adept in the art of foxing.

Contemplating the best place to give his man an opportunity for slipping away, while being able to follow him fairly easily, he decided on the Embankment, and walked down Villiers Street towards Charing Cross Underground Station. Towards the end of the street the man made his effort.

Again he showed a well-developed cunning.

They were ten yards from Hungerford Bridge when he slipped out of Mike's loose hold, and made for the wooden steps leading to the foot-bridge. A dozen people stared uncertainly, while Errol waited for a few seconds, as if so taken by surprise that he could not immediately get into action.

Then he followed.

He reached the bend at the far end of the bridge, swerved round it, saw his quarry nearly at the end of the slope which ran to the mean little streets behind Waterloo Station, and knew that when the man reached the street at the end he could go in one of three directions.

He increased his pace.

He made good progress, for he saw his man turning into a narrow road which led straight to the station. Still running like the wind, the little man glanced over his shoulder.

It was possible that he was going to make a train journey, but more likely that he had chosen Waterloo because of its diversity of hiding-places.

As he followed the little man into the station, Mike wished that there had been someone else with him, and while the wish was expressing itself in his mind he heard a thin voice say:

'Want any help, sir?'

He turned abruptly; and looked down into the wide blue eyes of the ginger-haired office boy.

'I thought he might give you the slip, sir. He's just gone into the cloak-room.'

'Good man. Watch it, will you? There's only one way out, and we're bound to see him. I want to make a telephone call—if he comes up, make a sign to me and I'll be with you.'

Mike hurried to a nearby telephone kiosk, dialled a Mayfair number, and waited impatiently.

'Davidson here.' said a languid voice at the other end.

'Wally, I need help.' said Mike, spelling his name backwards in the usual way. 'I'm at Waterloo, the end opposite the cinema. How soon can you get here?'

'I'm nearly there,' said Wally Davidson.

Mike returned to the boy, who looked up at him hopefully.

'Nothing doing, sir, but I've had an idea. Supposing I go in and see what he's up to?'

'I'd better go, old man,' said Mike reasoningly. 'He's a tough customer.'

'You're telling *me*,' said the boy with a grin. 'But he won't spot me!'

Mike hesitated.

'Okay?' demanded the boy eagerly.

'Right you are, my son! Don't hang about, just see whether he's in the barber's saloon, or the washroom.'

'O-*kay!*' said the boy and scampered off. When he came back his face was showing satisfaction and surprise. He hurried towards Mike.

'He's having a haircut,' he said breathlessly. 'I saw him in the mirror. Half of his hair is on, half off; strewth, he don't half look different.'

'Oh-h,' said Mike slowly. 'Sonny, you're being very valuable indeed, and I'm glad you came along. I'm expecting a friend in a few minutes, and he'll be able to take over from us. When he arrives, I'll introduce you, you'll point out our man, and then get away.'

'Okay,' said the boy. 'What then? There must be *something* I can do. I've been useful; you said it yourself.'

'You've been A.1,' said Mike, and he had not the heart to say there was nothing more that the boy could do. 'All right, come along to see me later in the day. If I'm not in, try Number 55g Brook Street—a few doors along from my flat.' He handed the boy a card, which declared him to reside at 39j Brook Street. The boy read the card eagerly, then took out a tattered-looking wallet, and carefully stowed away the precious slip of pasteboard.

Mike glanced towards the head of the steps, and relief dawned, for he saw Wally Davidson approaching.

Davidson was a tall man, and very thin. His features were good and, but for a longer nose than average, he would have justified the description of handsome. His eyes were filled with a languid amusement as he approached, and although he walked at a good pace he contrived to create an impression of laziness. In their less original moments, the Department agents christened Davidson 'Weary Wally'.

But he would boast, on occasions, that he carried more scars on his person—five in all, including three in the chest— than any other of Craigie's men. He was one of Craigie's oldest agents in years of service, and was nearer forty than thirty, although his thinness and his expression gave him an ageless appearance.

He raised his right hand, lethargically.

'Hallo, hallo! How's tricks?'

'Tricky,' said Mike promptly. 'Wally, be serious for a moment, and meet—' He hesitated. 'What's your name?'

'Jimmy Mayo,' said the boy, eyeing Wally eagerly.

'Jimmy Mayo, who's been invaluable,' said Mike. 'He'll tell you of a little man we want followed. Just trail him home, if you can, and let G.C. have a report.'

'Ah,' said Wally, looking down at Jimmy. 'A budding detective, eh? Catch 'em young; that's the spirit.' He saw Jimmy's chest swell, and Mike blessed Wally for his quick appreciation of the position. 'All right, Mike.'

'I'll be seeing you,' said Mike, and he left the tall man and Jimmy together.

Crossing Hungerford Bridge, he noticed two heavily-built men approaching him. It was not until they had nearly reached him that he was aware of danger.

He backed quickly away.

He avoided a swinging blow to his face, but could not avoid the arms of the other man, which suddenly gripped his knees, and lifted him, until he felt himself on a level with the parapet. A vicious punch to the stomach winded him, making him gasp.

And then he went over the parapet, and into the river below.

5

COLD WATER

C old and clammy, the river closed about Mike Erroll. He had his eyes shut tightly, felt the pressure at his chest growing insupportable.

Then his head broke the surface.

The water was smooth, and he could see the warehouses on the one side and the Embankment on the other, with the tall buildings beyond, and the white edifice of Shell House almost on a level with him. By then he was swimming more strongly. He watched for any craft in mid-river, but saw none, although on the Surrey side there were barges and tug-boats moored by the dozen. All at once he heard a staccato note, and knew that a motor-boat was somewhere near.

He saw it after a few seconds.

It was approaching him from the Middlesex bank, two men in uniform standing in it, one with a rope in his hands. Soon the rope hissed through the air, falling with a dull plop close beside him, only to be carried out of his reach.

A second effort was successful.

By the time the boat was moored to a landing stage by Hungerford Bridge he was feeling very much better. The two policemen had said nothing, but one of them turned towards him.

'Don't you think we've got enough to do without fishing for people like you?'

Mike stared. '"People like me?"'

'Well, sir,' said the policeman, 'throwing yourself over the bridge like that isn't done by *accident*. A day in a cell and a visit to the Court in the morning will make you realise you can't waste public time and money.'

Mike spoke more crisply.

'You're quite right, officer, that was no accident. But a word with Superintendent Miller, of the Yard, will reassure you, I fancy.'

The name of Superintendent Miller caused a certain flutter, and Mike was driven direct to Scotland Yard. After he had waited ten minutes inside the courtyard, the policeman who had admonished him came hurrying out, full of apologies, and a few moments later Mike was back in the police car and on his way to Brook Street.

Although little more than forty minutes had passed from the time he had been pushed over the parapet to the moment when he opened the door of his flat and went through, it seemed like several hours.

The flat was empty, and he went into the bathroom, running the hot water while he stripped off his sodden clothes. He soaked himself for twenty minutes, then dressed, lit a cigarette, and considered the position.

He was still considering it when footsteps sounded by the front door, which opened to admit first Mark, then Loftus. Mike did not stand up, but waved a hand.

'Just when I was thinking of calling Craigie,' he said. 'I wondered if you two were all right. I—' he broke off, frowning, for just as earlier there had been something odd about Bill Loftus, he now recognised the same thing in his cousin.

Loftus asked sharply:

'Did you follow him?'

'Not all the way, I—'

'Why the devil can't you do a job when you get one?' demanded Mark Errol.

A sharp retort was on Mike's tongue; he hardly knew why he held it back, speaking instead with commendable mildness.

'I got as far as Waterloo, and he went to have a hair-cut. I sent for Wally, and left the job to him—our little man wouldn't know Wally. Of course, I could have kept on him myself and thus made sure he would walk London all day rather than go anywhere that mattered, but the Wally angle seemed best.'

Loftus looked relieved.

'And rightly, Mike. What happened?'

Mike said gently: 'I left Wally and Jimmy at Waterloo—'

'Jimmy who?'

'Mayo.' Mike hid a smile, explained, and saw Loftus's lips relax in a quick smile of amusement. But even that was not as appreciative as might be expected, and Mike's curiosity was working overtime. But he continued in a vein of facetiousness.

'Then I walked back over Hungerford Bridge, and had a swim.'

'Don't drag it out, Mike. This is serious.'

'Oh,' said Mike slowly. So there *was* something wrong. He finished his story fully but without trimmings.

'Bad show,' said Mark, clearly regretting his earlier ill-temper. 'You're sure you're all right?'

'I'm as right as a trivet, but what the devil is getting you fellows down? There's a pall of gloom which you could cut with a knife.'

'Easy,' said Loftus, playing with a button of his coat, 'Mark will tell you. It doesn't concern this business, although it arises from it.' He stepped to the window and looked out, talking while his back was towards the others.

'You didn't get a thorough look at the brace who attacked you?'

'No,' said Mike regretfully.

'Had you seen either of them before?'

'No, they weren't on the bridge the first time. Y'know,' went on Mike, 'it's a bit of a puzzle. Supposing I'd gone by cab from Waterloo? After all, the bridge was the last route I was likely to take, wasn't it? I don't really know why I decided to walk back again, unless it was that I thought I'd be able to sort things out a bit better when walking. I—what's bitten you?' he added abruptly, for Loftus snapped his fingers sharply, then stepped to the telephone.

He was dialling a number as Mike spoke.

'We're dumb,' Loftus said sharply. 'You were known because you were followed. In other words, you and the little man were followed. Presumably there were more than two men, and each route from the station was guarded. That suggests'—there was more than a hint of excitement in Loftus's voice as he went on—'considerable numbers, my hearties! A young army must have been collected about Waterloo, and you were covered all the way. They wanted to kill you, obviously.'

'Why?' said Mike helplessly. 'Damn it, the man got away.'

'They still wanted *you*,' said Loftus. 'Why you in particular doesn't much matter, but we'll find out.'

'*I'm* quite interested in the reason,' said Mike mildly.

Loftus grinned; he looked more normal than at any time since entering the flat, but he did not go on. Instead:

'Scotland Yard—Superintendent Miller, please, wanted by Bill Loftus.' He waited, an eyebrow raised, until a distorted sound came from the telephone. 'Miller?' he asked. 'Good man. This is urgent—will you put a call out for Wally Davidson? Not to be brought in, but to be traced and followed . . . yes, our Wally . . . and if you let me know the moment there's any news I'll be extremely grateful . . . many thanks.'

He rang off, and swung round to the others.

'Mike was closely watched, and was therefore seen at Waterloo. Probably Wally was also seen, and may well have been followed. So might the infant, but our watchful gentlemen might possibly give him the go-by.'

Mike stared.

'Good God! If they get Wally we're in the cart.'

'It won't be so good,' said Loftus. Despite the risks inherent in the situation there was a compressed excitement in him which the others knew well. 'But what *is* good is the evidence of numbers. There is a strong branch of the organisation here, an organisation, if my guess is right, which is concentrating on developing isolationism in the States. I think I'll get over and see Craigie again. As soon as there's anything you can do, I'll call you.' He smiled briefly, then went out, moving very quickly and with an unusual quietness.

The door closed.

Mike looked at Mark, and said:

'What *is* the matter with him?'

There was a short pause; then Mark told his cousin about Diana's death. As he did so, the expression on Mike Errol's face altered, and grew bleak.

It was a bleakness which was to come to every member of

33

Department Z who, in the next few days, heard what had happened to Diana Woodward.

Meanwhile, Loftus saw Craigie, and the two men discussed every possible angle of the situation. Craigie telephoned Miller twice, but there was no report of Davidson. That did not necessarily mean that Wally had disappeared, but it did imply that his chase had led him outside London. At Loftus's request, the Yard widened the scope of the inquiries, but as the minutes ticked slowly by and no news came in, Loftus grew more and more worried.

The two men had finished their discussion, and Loftus was just getting to his feet, when a slight clicking sound was followed by a green light at the mantelshelf. Only men who knew Craigie well were aware of the existence of the concealed press-button outside which operated this light. Loftus looked towards the door as it opened, and started with surprise as Hershall entered.

He nodded to Loftus abruptly, and looked at Craigie.

'I've found you both at the same time, have I?' He sat on the arm of Loftus's chair, pushing him down when he started to get up. 'Sit down, Loftus, and don't fidget.' He paused, lighting a cheroot and tossing the match into the fireplace, looking into the bright embers intently. The muscles of his cheeks moved a little, his brows were drawn together. Neither Craigie nor Loftus had seen the Prime Minister in such a mood. 'Well you'd better have it. Certain quarters suggest that our Secret Service sabotaged that plane. Diana Woodward was recognised. She was to have left the plane at an intermediate stop but the bomb exploded too soon. That's the tale and some Americans will believe it.'

Loftus sat stunned as Hershall went on:

'Loftus, I've had reason to be grateful to you in the past, and to the whole Department. But you have never, I think, faced so urgent and imperative a problem. What is being threatened is the whole fabric of Anglo-American friendship. I don't need to say more. You can do exactly what you like; I've told Craigie that. If it is possible to stop the trouble in this country, do so. Let nothing get in your way, whatever it may be.'

Hershall stopped, looked from one man to the other, nodded and stepped to the door. As it slid at Craigie's touch on the switch, Hershall looked over his shoulder.

'You'll do what you can, I know. Keep me informed.'

Then he went out.

There was no doubting the grim seriousness of the Prime Minister's words. Loftus lit a cigarette, and flicked the match towards the fireplace, drumming his fingers on the arm of his chair as he said:

'Well, that's that. You'll send a general call out to everyone?'

'It's gone,' said Craigie. 'It's a good time as far as that is concerned, we've more than fifty men in the country. They should all be ready by now.'

'Good,' said Loftus. He drew his chair nearer to Craigie's desk, and the two men went still further into the preparations for the fight against what was, so far, little more than a shadow.

It was an hour or so later before Loftus left Craigie's office and made his way homewards. As he turned into Brook Street, he saw a lad cycling towards him, and although this lad was not in uniform, he reminded Loftus vividly of the boy who had delivered Diana's cable. He tightened his lips as he walked on, but the cyclist came wobbling towards him. Loftus paid him closer attention.

The lad fell off his machine.

Loftus muttered an exclamation and hurried forward. The cyclist, stretched out on the ground, made no attempt to get up. He was deathly pale, and there was a rough bandage about his right hand, a nasty graze at his right temple. There was a wealth of appeal in his eyes as Loftus bent over him.

Loftus said:

'This won't do, Jimmy Mayo! What have you been doing; getting into trouble?'

'You—you got—got to hurry,' said Jimmy very softly; then he fainted.

6

REGULAR FELLOW

L oftus lifted the cycle away, then bent down and raised the boy in his arms. Several people came up, including a constable. Loftus turned towards him.

'Tell Dr. Little that I'd like to see him at once, will you?'

The constable, who knew Loftus well, and had learned that what Loftus said was as good as an order from Superintendent Miller, saluted and hurried along Brook Street, at the far end of which lived Dr. Little, who had at one time been on the active list of Craigie's men. Little arrived at Loftus's flat very soon after Loftus had rested the lad on a bed in the spare room, and went to his task gently and dexterously. Once or twice he grunted under his breath. Loftus meanwhile prepared hot water, a sponge, and a towel. He carried them into the bedroom as Little glanced up.

'Damned shame, *damned* shame. What unmentionable brutes would shoot a child of this age?'

'Shoot?' exclaimed Loftus.

'Yes,' said Little. 'Two bullets, high in the shoulder. Don't know how the little chap managed to get here. That bag, please—' He began to cleanse the wounds.

'How soon can you get him round?' asked Loftus.

'I don't know,' said Little gruffly. 'How urgent is it?'

'It couldn't be more important.'

'H'm. He'll come round soon, I think, and I'll give him a sleeping draught when you've finished. Make it easy for him.'

As he finished speaking, Jimmy opened his eyes. The boy's gaze roved about the room, then settled on Loftus. His lips worked, and he spoke in a barely audible voice.

'Hurry—hurry—your friend—they took him away. I—I came back to report.'

'Stout fellow,' said Loftus. 'Where did they take him?'

'Got—got it written down,' said Jimmy. 'Back—back of the c-card—'

He moved his left hand weakly towards his coat pocket. Loftus slid out the tattered wallet, and the lad nodded. Loftus ran through the papers, mostly foreign stamps stuck on sadly-soiled envelopes, then came across a new-looking white card. He read Mike Errol's address and then, on the reverse side, a scrawled note in pencil:

18 Galloway Road,
Barnes.

Loftus looked down on the drawn face with a smile.

'You're a regular fellow, and we won't forget this. All right, Doc. Jimmy, you'll have a longish sleep and when you wake up I'd like a full report. Meanwhile. I'll look after the others without losing time.'

'O-kay,' said Jimmy, slowly and wearily. He closed his eyes.

Loftus stepped to the telephone and dialled three numbers, giving precisely the same instructions to the three men who answered him, men to whom he introduced himself by the reverse spelling of his name.

Then Mike and Mark arrived.

Loftus paused with a hand on the receiver.

'Mark, use the other 'phone and call Grey, Dunster and Lettinson—they're to go, armed, to within a hundred yards of 18 Galloway Road, Barnes, and wait for me.'

Mike's eyes glistened, while his cousin started immediately for the second telephone. Loftus and Mark dialled numbers in quick succession, giving instructions. When they had finished, Loftus went towards the bedroom.

'There'll be ten waiting for us, and thirteen, with us, to make the unlucky number. You've got guns?'

Mike and Mark nodded.

Loftus took two Webley automatics from a drawer in the wardrobe, then hurried after the others, who were waiting for him by the main door of the flat. His Jaguar was at a garage not far away, and as they neared the garage they met Oundle.

'Hail,' said Oundle, sepulchrally but without enthusiasm. 'Gordon sent me on a wild goose chase, Bill, and I didn't like it.'

'You'll like where I'm going to take you, I hope,' said Loftus.

They were driving over Barnes Common when he had finished bringing them up to date.

The others made little comment, although Mike Errol in particular was thinking of Jimmy Mayo. Loftus, looking straight ahead of him, opened out into a burst of speed which made the Common seem like a suburban back garden, and pulled up with a squealing of brakes opposite a policeman, who gazed at him with reproach.

'Good evening, constable,' said Loftus crisply. 'Galloway Road, please.'

The policeman stared. '*Ga*lloway Road?'

'That's right,' said Loftus. 'Is it strange?'

'Well, sir.' A thick forefinger rubbed a flattened nose. 'I wouldn't say *that*. But you're the *seventh* gentleman to ask me in the past twenty minutes; after the third, I started to count.'

Loftus's eyes creased at the corners.

'Well, well! There are going to be ructions there I think, constable.' Loftus showed his Special Branch card, and the man's eyes widened; he saluted, gave the necessary directions, and asked if there was anything more he could do.

'Generally speaking, no,' said Loftus. 'But you can keep your eyes open and if there seems to be any need for help, weigh in.' He spoke more to make the policeman happy than because he thought there could be any call on his services.

Galloway Road turned out to be one of those strange dead ends, dotted with cottages here and large houses there, without apparent design or reason.

Immediately past No. 18, the road narrowed to a track barely wide enough for the car. The track was rough, and sloped sharply. Beyond it, and the high fence on either side, Loftus could see the silver surface of the Thames, and the trees on the far side of the river.

He pulled the car up outside the house, which was large and rambling. The garden was unkempt; the soil had not been turned for years, and the lawns had been allowed to grow into seed, and then lie fallow. There was a powerful stench of rotting vegetation.

'H'm,' said Mike. 'I suppose Jimmy didn't make a mistake?'

'He did not,' said Loftus. 'Cars have been here, and in the past few hours. Our other fellows are doing well, aren't they?'

'Why?' asked Mark.

'We haven't seen a sign of them,' said Loftus. 'But the bobby said they were here. Mark, you go in that direction, Mike, you go in this, and tell them to close in. Ned and I will try the house itself.'

The Errols knew better than to argue, although they were in telepathic agreement, thinking that Loftus would be well advised to approach with greater care than it seemed he was proposing. But Loftus opened the wide wooden gates, blocked them with stones, and then rejoined Oundle in the Jaguar, swinging the car round into the drive.

He pulled up outside the front door.

'Nice work,' said Ned Oundle. 'If they'd wanted a stab at us, you made it too fast for them. What's next?'

Loftus screwed up his eyes.

'I—don't—know,' he said slowly. 'The place seems too neglected to have been in use very much. It looks as if we might be on another white elephant, old son.' He was clearly afraid that that was so, and Oundle had rarely seen him look more disappointed. But Loftus tightened his lips, went up the three stone steps, and then rapped loudly on the peeling front door. The iron knocker was rusted over, as was the letter-box.

A hollow echo sounded from inside the house.

Loftus tried again, but there was no response. He shrugged, waiting for a few minutes, until Mike and Mark appeared, hurrying up the drive. They reported that the house was surrounded by Department men at close quarters.

Loftus turned.

'Check if there's a side entrance as well,' he told them, 'and if there is, one of you stay there, the other stay by the back.' He was drawing on a glove as he spoke and, on his last word, he drove his clenched fist through a panel of frosted glass in the front door.

The crack of the splintering panel, and the tinkling of glass falling both inside and outside, were the only sounds which followed him.

He pushed his arm through the hole, found the catch, and slid it back. The door opened easily, and he and Ned Oundle stepped into a lofty, empty hall. There were cobwebs and there was dust, but there was no evidence of occupation—or there seemed not to be, until Loftus bent down and picked up from the floor the squashed stub of a cigarette.

The end was damp.

'Yes, it's been occupied recently,' he said, 'but it looks like a rendezvous of convenience, and they probably haven't left much behind.'

'What about Wally?' asked Mike, who had forced an entrance through the back door, closely followed by Mark.

'He could be here,' admitted Loftus. 'I'll take the upper rooms, with Ned. You two make what you can of the ground floor and cellars, if any.'

He started up the wide, uncarpeted stairs, distributing dust with every step, and seeing ahead of him the evidence of other footsteps. It was impossible to judge how many people had been in the house recently, but from the cluster of footprints in the dust on the first landing the number had been considerable.

Paper was peeling from the landing walls and from the walls of every room they went into. Now and again they could hear the murmur of voices from below stairs; sounds carried a long way in the emptiness of Number 18, and even their own breathing seemed loud. They did not speak as they went from room to room, finding the same desolate prospect each time.

'No go,' said Ned at last.

Loftus shrugged. 'We'll see. There's another floor.'

He had seen a third set of windows from the street, but they did not find the staircase leading to the second floor for some minutes. Eventually they discovered that it led from a small room which they had nearly missed, the outer door of which was papered to match the wall, and not easily discernible.

Climbing up the staircase, which was steep and gloomy, they reached a narrow landing, from which three doors led, each of them shut. Together they approached the first. It opened easily, revealing yet another dusty, empty room. Then they tried the handles of the second and third doors, but these remained firm.

Loftus played with the handle of the second door for some seconds, and then shrugged.

'Bolted, I think. We'll try this one first.'

He drew back, then launched his vast frame against the door. It quivered violently, and the crash echoed about the landing and went even further, for faintly from below there came a cry:

'You—all—right?' It was Mark or Mike.

'Yes!' called Ned.

Once again Loftus threw his weight against the door, and this time it offered little resistance, swinging inwards with a loud splintering noise.

The room was not empty.

There was a camp bed in one corner, a chair and a small table. By the table was a decanter of water, and several books, although what use either books or water were likely to be to the occupant of the bed they did not know.

Loftus and Ned stared, for perhaps ten seconds. Then they were both galvanised into action, reaching the bedside at the same time.

Looking at them with wide open eyes, eyes filled with alarm, was a girl; her mouth covered with a tightly-drawn scarf, her body bound securely to the bed.

7

'UP SHE GOES'

Loftus smiled down at the girl.

'You'll be all right,' he said, and the nonchalant nature of the words, together with the transforming effect of his smile, were both calculated to reassure her. He added:

'Untie her, Ned. I'm going next door.'

He tried to empty his mind of the dread possibilities which the discovery engendered as he went on to the landing again, and there saw Mike Errol. Mike's hair was ruffled, and there was a cobweb smeared across his ears to his chin. His hands were blackened as if with coaldust, and there was a dark patch on the knee of his right trouser-leg.

'There's nothing below,' he said.

Loftus didn't speak, but turned his attention to the third door. This time it gave way at the first onslaught, and he was precipitated into the room.

He put a hand to the floor to save himself from complete disaster, and straightened up; but the assault had carried him half-way across the room, and before he stood upright he kicked against a man lying on the floor.

It was Wally Davidson.

His coat was torn, his collar undone, and he was bound and gagged. Dust and dirt were all over him, and grimed on to his face by perspiration which had poured from his forehead and then dried.

Loftus freed his mouth, which had been secured by a neck-tie, drawn very tightly. The corners of his lips, and parts of his cheeks, were red and inflamed, and Wally gulped two or three times while trying to speak. He made no sound but an incoherent muttering.

Loftus said: 'Hold it, old man.'

Wally had his mouth half-open, and Loftus inserted a finger and slowly prised out a small handkerchief, rolled into a ball and now sodden with saliva. Wally retched, and after a few seconds began to breathe very heavily.

'Gerrow, gerrow?' he muttered, nodding violently towards the door. 'Gerrow, gerrow, blow-ar, blow-ar.' His eyes rolled, and he nodded to the door yet again, with a desperation which in itself would have told Loftus what was the matter.

Wally was trying to say:

'Get out—blow up.'

Loftus rose to his feet bent down, and with no great effort lifted Wally bodily from the floor. He reached the door as Mike appeared, empty-handed.

'We're getting out,' Loftus snapped. 'Tell Ned, and make it fast.'

He went as quickly as he could to the top of the stairs. Before he reached the small room from which the staircase led, Mike was coming after him, carrying the girl, with Ned Oundle close behind him. They reached the main landing, and went down the wide staircase at good speed, Loftus warning the others what was likely to happen. As they reached the porch Loftus saw two men in a tangle of shrubs and long grass near the drive. He recognized his own agents, and raised his voice to a stentorian bellow which must have reached the ears of anyone within a hundred yards radius.

'Get away from here!'

The two men disappeared, and there were sounds of rustling and running from all about the grounds. In a matter of seconds, more men appeared, as if from nowhere, climbed to the top of the fence which surrounded the house, and dropped to the other side.

Reaching the Jaguar, which he had left with its nose pointing towards the gate, Loftus pushed Wally into the back seat, then slipped behind the wheel. Ned got in beside him. Mike bundled the girl in with Wally, then got in beside Ned. The engine purred into life.

The car was just outside the gate, and turning into Galloway Road, when it happened.

The roar was devastating, shattering against the eardrums, deafening them. The blast, following a split-second later, lifted the car two feet from the ground, and although it landed on all four wheels Loftus was afraid for a moment that it would be out of control. But the engine did not stop, and he managed to keep it on the roadway.

He half-turned his head—*and saw 18 Galloway Road going up into the air.*

It did not go in one piece, although for the first moment it seemed as if that was happening. It broke up, like a pack of stacked cards, and then the pieces went higher and wider. Small objects began to fall about the road and the car. Men who had hurried away at Loftus's shout were flung to the ground, glass broke up and down the road, a piece of granite from Number 18 fell between one of the flattened men and a lamp-post, bounced, and sent the lamppost flat but missed the man.

Something tore through the wind-screen, and for some seconds there was a constant rattle on the wings and the body. The roar of the explosion seemed to be in their ears for a long time, but finally it faded, leaving only a drumming; the hail of debris stopped.

Loftus accelerated desperately. He had to be clear before the explosion brought the residents of Galloway Road out to investigate.

They reached Brook Street in half-an-hour, and by this time both Wally and the girl had recovered sufficiently to be able to walk up the stairs. In the last ten minutes of the drive Wally had talked, although he had little enough constructive information.

He had followed the man whom Jimmy Mayo had pointed out to him, had trailed him as far as Galloway Road, then after making a survey of No. 18, had turned towards the nearest telephone kiosk. Before he had reached it he had been cracked on the head, and remembered little more; although he did recall seeing flashes from what he thought were silenced guns.

Mike told him how Jimmy had given the alarm.

Wally's eyes widened.

'Game little beggar,' he said. 'We owe him a lot—and I owe him even more.'

'The country might owe him plenty, too,' said Loftus, and this time could look at the girl without risk, for the car was parked outside the flat.

Upstairs, a policeman was waiting. He saluted, and reported that arrangements had been made for the patient to go to a nursing home, and would Mr. Loftus get in touch with the doctor?

'Yes, I will,' said Loftus. 'Thanks a lot, constable.'

'That's all right, sir. Glad to be of service.' The man knew Loftus and his friends well enough to show no particular curiosity. 'Like me to stay here, sir? I've been detailed to do anything you want.'

'That's a good idea,' said Loftus. 'Wait on the landing, will you?'

Inside the flat, he looked at the girl evenly. She was tall, only five or six inches shorter than his six-feet-three.

'Ned, show Miss—,' he paused.

'My name is Weston,' said the girl quietly.

'Show Miss Weston next door, will you? She'll be glad to tidy up.'

All of the regular Department men present were surprised by that request, for the flat next to Loftus's had, at one time, been occupied by Diana. A special communicating door had been made between the two flats, connecting the respective landings. Since Diana had left for America, Loftus had maintained it in readiness for her return.

It was a considerable effort now, for him to let this strange girl walk into her flat.

But it was useless, he told himself, to brood, to overdo the sentimentality. The air disaster had happened, and he had to look forward, not backward. The flat was there, and it might as well be used. The girl needed half-an-hour to wash, use powder and lipstick; her own was badly smeared. As she started towards the door, with Ned, Loftus smiled and said:

'You'll find most of the things you'll need, I think.'

'Thank—thank you.' She was a little uncertain of herself, which was hardly surprising. Loftus did not watch her go out of the lounge, but stepped to a cabinet, opened it, and took out whiskey. Mike, Mark and Wally were all equally glad of a drink. Loftus, usually very sparing, took a strong one. He lit a cigarette, pursed his lips, then said evenly:

'Well, our main hope is the girl. Had you seen her before, Wally?'

'No,' said Wally.

'You'd no idea she was there?'

'None at all.'

'H'm. How did you know about the blow-up?'

'I heard two of the swine talking, Bill. They were a tough bunch, one way and the other. By tough I mean rough-necks. They apparently knew just what they were doing, and there was some talk about a fuse, and watching from the tow-path— you reached that from the end of the street, perhaps you noticed.'

'Yes,' said Loftus. His eyes narrowed and he considered that interesting item of information. The street had been watched, and the explosion timed for the moment he was inside the house. Clearly Jimmy Mayo's escape had been realised in its full significance, and the 'rough-necks' had tried to turn it to their full advantage.

He could go a step further.

The explosives must have been buried at the house for some time, suggesting that sooner or later it had been planned to lure him and the others to the house. Jimmy had forestalled the move, that was all.

A ring at the door broke into his train of thought. Mike went to open it. Standing squarely across the threshold, and effectively blocking the entrance, was the policeman who had been left on duty on the landing. A tall, distinguished looking man was trying to get past him. It was Cyrus Hoppermann.

'Excuse me, sir,' said the constable. 'There's a gentleman here who says—'

'Loftus, what absurd nonsense is this?' demanded the American.

Loftus said evenly: 'All right, officer, thanks. But stop anyone else who wants to come through, just as you have this gentleman. Come in, Hoppermann.'

The American made no attempt to cover his annoyance.

'Do you always make a habit of guarding your front door?' he demanded.

'Can you think of any reason why I shouldn't?' asked Loftus coldly. 'The man had orders, and obeyed them. Why try to get past him? If you reckoned on the surprise effect of your call, you needn't have troubled. Now, what can I do for you?'

'I—I want your advice,' Hoppermann said with apparent reluctance.

'That's surprising,' said Loftus. 'I advised you to stay at the Embassy, but you rejected the suggestion. Are you likely to be more attentive to anything else?'

He stopped suddenly, as the communicating door between the two flats swung open. The girl stepped through, and even in that moment Loftus saw enough to realise that her appearance had been transformed by skillful attention. But that faded into insignificance as Hoppermann looked towards her and then stared, wide-eyed, his lips parted.

'Christine! What are *you* doing here?'

There was a slight pause, and then Christine Weston said: 'Hallo, father.'

She spoke without warmth or enthusiasm.

8

CHRISTINE

The initial shock of that brief exchange soon passed. Loftus stepped forward toward the girl.

'I don't need to introduce you, I can see.'

Hoppermann turned on him.

'What is this, Loftus? What is my daughter doing here? Are you endeavouring to pry into my private affairs?'

Loftus smiled faintly.

'Not yet,' he said. 'Miss—'

'She's not Miss,' snapped Hoppermann.

'I'm sorry. *Mrs.* Weston came here quite by chance, needing a little assistance.'

'I don't believe it,' said Hoppermann flatly.

'That's too bad,' said Loftus.

There was an awkward pause, then Hoppermann raised his hands helplessly.

'This is absurd, Loftus. We are always at cross-purposes. I have been given to understand that you are more likely to be able to help me than anyone else, but how can I ask for your assistance if you are continually obstructive?'

Loftus smiled freely.

'It is a bit difficult, isn't it? After all, you're prejudiced against us, and I've returned the compliment. But we can forget that for the time being. I was just going to talk with Mrs. Weston, but if you're in a hurry—'

'I can hear what she has to say, surely.'

Loftus eyed the girl.

She nodded, and there was a faint smile on her lips; she had a very well-shaped mouth. Her hair was dark, and in the last few moments she had contrived not only to make it tidy, but to bring a wave to it, with a glossy sheen which was very attractive.

Her wrists were bandaged, half-covered by the long sleeves of a flowered frock, which Loftus recognized as Diana's.

Then he saw that she wore a solitaire engagement ring and a slim circlet of white gold or platinum. He did not know why he had been surprised to learn that she was married.

'Well, let's get comfortable,' he said.

Ushering them into the sitting-room, he glanced at his watch. It was half-past seven, thus explaining the fact that he felt ravenously hungry. He sent the others out for a meal; it was probable that both Hoppermann and his daughter would talk more freely to him alone.

He offered cigarettes; the girl refused, but Hoppermann took one.

With smoke curling towards the ceiling, Loftus spoke.

'I'm not going to tell you how I discovered that 18 Galloway Road was of interest,' he told the girl, 'nor what led up to the visit. I'll just say that I did discover it, went there, and found you a prisoner.'

Hoppermann ejaculated: 'What's that?'

Loftus explained briefly. Hoppermann's eyes widened, and Loftus had a feeling that the man was jolted badly. He acted with a naiveté not to be expected from a man of authority and affairs.

'What on earth happened to you, Christine?' Hoppermann demanded as Loftus finished.

'I hardly know, even now,' she said slowly. 'I was at my flat and somebody rang the bell. When I answered the door there were two men outside—one of them pushed a wad of something over my face, and I passed out.'

'This is fantastic!' said Hoppermann.

'Did they ask you any questions?' Loftus said. 'After the passing-out stage, I mean.'

She smiled a little. 'Yes, plenty—about my father. Where was he likely to be, where had I arranged to meet him—those, and a lot more. As I didn't know he was in England, and wasn't likely to want to see him anyway—nor he me, for that matter—I couldn't tell them much. They grew hot-tempered, I guess, and I thought I was in for a bad time, but then they tied me up and gagged me.' She glanced at her wrists and frowned, but made no further comment.

Loftus said slowly: 'Well, we've a good explanation of that, I think. She was wanted to give details of your movements over here, Hoppermann. And there was probably an idea that she could be used to coerce you.'

Hoppermann frowned, and ran his fingers along his jaw.

'You won't need telling, Loftus, that Christine and I are not on good terms. We disagreed about—'

'I'll tell him,' said the girl. She turned to Loftus. 'Father disapproved of me marrying an Englishman. He had been continuously disapproving of everything I wanted to do myself for twenty-seven years, and I grew tired of it.' She paused, losing a little of her colour. 'My husband was killed in a car accident. Since then, I've been living in London.'

Hoppermann frowned.

53

'The main point of difference was your marriage, and you know it. He was—' The man paused, and coloured slightly. 'Loftus, I had nothing against Christine's husband, except that I disapproved of his mode of life. I may have been wrong—' he brushed his hand over his forehead, and Loftus thought there was a hint of appeal in his eyes as he looked at his daughter. 'Christine, you'll always be welcome back home. Your mother grieves for you.'

Loftus broke a short silence.

'Well, we know why Mrs. Weston was taken away, I think. Why did you come to see me, Hoppermann?'

'I've talked at the Embassy, and our own people say that if anyone can solve this mystery, you can. I've already explained to you that I need to take a look at England, and must be back after seven days. It's clear that I'll need protection, and I want yours, Loftus. Can you arrange that?'

Loftus shrugged. 'I'm not my own master you know. And I'm busy as it is.'

'You can arrange it if you will.'

'I don't think so,' said Loftus. 'But I'll put it up to my superiors, and discuss it with them.'

'How soon will you know?'

'By midnight.'

'What do you advise me to do until then?'

'Go back to the Embassy and stay there,' said Loftus grimly. 'And if I were you I'd take Mrs. Weston with you. She'll be safer there than anywhere else—besides, she'll probably be able to tell you of some of the places where we need American help, *and* where we can help America—even though some people *do* seem to think we're useless. Internal differences in America now can be disastrous, and internal differences will develop if the isolationists are able to get the backing of enough influential industrialists. But—' he raised a hand as

Hoppermann tried to interrupt. 'But it goes deeper than that. It's quite clear that powerful efforts are being made to prejudice American public opinion. Efforts appear to be directed against you, (a) to prevent you from seeing the truth, and (b) to create the impression in America that you were stopped by British agents. The effect of the latter will be enormous, if it succeeds.'

As he had been speaking the girl's eyes had widened, and he saw her gripping the arms of her chair. Hoppermann was also looking at him wide-eyed, and appeared to be impressed. But it was Christine who spoke first.

'It's infamous. It mustn't happen.'

'It won't if we can help it,' said Loftus. He smiled quickly, and stood up. 'Now I must have some food, I haven't had a square meal to-day, and after that I must get busy. Shall I find you at the Embassy, Hoppermann?'

'Yes, I'll be there.'

'And Mrs. Weston?'

She shrugged. 'I'll dine there, if it can be arranged.'

'Good,' said Loftus. 'And in case I need to see you again, what is your usual address?'

'I'm at Bay Court, Park Lane,' said Christine. 'Number 120.'

Loftus saw them past the policeman on the landing, then returned to the sitting-room. From the window he noticed two Department Z agents, lounging in the street below, apparently with nothing better to do than glance from time to time at the evening papers. They looked up and saw him, and one nodded almost imperceptibly.

As Hoppermann and his daughter walked down the street, both agents fell in behind them.

And then, for the first time, Loftus saw the tall, thin man who, earlier in the day, had followed him and Hoppermann to the American Embassy. Loftus frowned, and started for the stairs; he was lucky, for the Errols were coming up.

'Mike,' said Loftus urgently. 'Grey and Dunster are following Hoppermann and the girl. There's a tall fellow with a bowler and an umbrella behind them. Watch him.'

'Right!' said Mike with alacrity, and he started down the stairs two at a time.

Loftus turned to Mark.

'I'm going to get some dinner and then have a word with Craigie. Hold the fort until I'm back, will you? What's happening to the others?'

'Wally's wrists are giving him trouble, and he's gone to see the doc. Ned went with him for safety.'

'H'm. They can't watch all of us all the time,' said Loftus.

He had a quick meal at a nearby restaurant, then hurried round to Craigie's office. Craigie looked up with a smile.

'Hallo, Bill, what's turned up?'

'A lot that isn't much,' said Loftus slowly, and he went through the afternoon's work. Craigie made notes in a short-hand which only he and Loftus understood.

'Has anything else developed?' asked Loftus.

Craigie tapped the stem of his meerschaum against his teeth.

'The howl is on, of course. No Press in the world would sit on the Hoppermann story unless it was forced to. It's suggested that Hoppermann chose a different route because England advised him to, on the strength of Communist agents wanting to make sure he didn't arrive.'

He broke off as the telephone rang, stood up and went to the desk. 'Hallo.' He paused, and then said: 'Yes, Mike, go on.'

Loftus stiffened; 'Mike' could only be Errol.

It was rare that Craigie's expression gave anything away,

and it did not do so now. But when he finished, with a decisive: 'Yes, at once,' he turned to Loftus and said quickly:

'They've got something. Hoppermann didn't go to the Embassy, he was driven to a house in Putney. Mike's waiting outside 4 Lester Drive, near the Heath.'

Loftus was already at the door.

'Putney, and next door to Barnes,' he said. 'That might give us something. Anything else?'

'Hoppermann was followed from the cab by a man who looked as though he were holding a gun in his pocket.'

'It could be true. Where did they pick up the cab?' 'It was standing at the corner of Brook Street and Piccadilly?'

'Standing there!' exclaimed Loftus. 'My God, must they walk into trouble? I'll ring you as soon as I can. Tell Ned and Mark to make it, will you?'

He went out, and hurried down the stairs, while Craigie lifted the telephone.

9

NOT NICE TO KNOW

Lester Drive was a long, straight road, leading from the Heath to Barnes, a fact which had already registered on Loftus's mind. Number 4 stood in half-an-acre of ground, and was surrounded by a five-feet high hedge of privet, trimly cut, as were the lawns and the shrubs on either side of the short drive.

The cab stopped outside, and Cyrus K. Hoppermann stepped out, with a man following him. The man poked an unseen object against his coat, and Hoppermann walked stiffly, looking very pale.

The cab went on; Mike, some fifty yards behind, did not see the girl. Between him and the house was a car containing Grey and Dunster.

In a small car which he had entered in Piccadilly was the tall man with the bowler hat, so that there was a collection of vehicles near 4 Lester Drive, and in Mike's opinion it was getting over-crowded. But there were times when it was quite impossible to keep their presence secret, and he saw no point in pretending secrecy then. He left his cab, telling the driver to wait for him at the end of the Drive, telephoned Craigie from a nearby call-box, then walked briskly up to Grey and Dunster.

After a short conference, Dunster hurried back to Mike's cab, and soon afterwards went in chase of the taxi in which, presumably, Christine Weston was still sitting. Grey in turn followed the man in the small car, which moved off without warning, and after some three minutes Mike found himself alone, without car or cab, and within twenty yards of the house into which Hoppermann had been persuaded. Mike was quite sure that, and without being nervous he was afraid there might be trouble directed against himself also, for his arrival must surely have been seen.

Dusk was falling over the commonland, and heavy clouds were gathered in the west, hiding the last rays of the sun behind them, making it dark before its time.

Mike looked at his watch; half-an-hour had passed since he had 'phoned Craigie, and there was surely a good chance of Loftus arriving at any moment. But before Loftus reached the Drive, Ned and Mark pulled up near Mike, who felt relieved that he was no longer on solitary duty.

'Anything?' demanded Mark cryptically.

'What do you know?' asked Mike.

'Nothing.'

Mike explained what he had seen, and the three men waited in the cover of a small cluster of bushes, the darkness falling about them, until soon it was safe for them to get nearer to Number 4.

Both inside and out, 4 Lester Drive was in excellent repair. It was, moreover, extremely well furnished, its owner, a Mr. Lewis, being a man possessing both wealth and good taste.

Three other people reached Number 4 that night. The Department Z men outside knew of their arrival, but could not see them well enough to identify them. Each rang the front door-bell, each was admitted by a sleek man-servant.

Lewis was sitting in the lounge hall, smoking a small cigar and reading an expensive American magazine, when his first caller was announced. He put the magazine down, and stood up gracefully.

'Good evening, Pellisser. I'm glad you were able to come.'

Pellisser was a short, thick-set man, with fleshy cheeks and jowl, well-dressed, obviously agitated.

'Have you got him?'

Lewis gave a faintly supercilious smile.

'He's on the premises.'

'Thank God for that,' said Pellisser, mopping his brow. 'I was beginning to think—'

What he was beginning to think did not transpire, for once again the sleek man-servant opened the door.

'Sir Geoffrey Gott.'

'Ah, Gott!' Lewis smiled as the second man entered, a man nearer sixty than fifty, grey-haired, red-faced, and more than inclined to plumpness. In his eyes was the same look of inquiry as Pellisser had betrayed.

'Where is he?'

'Quite safe, and here,' said Lewis.

Gott drew a deep breath, and brushed a hand across his forehead. His eyes turned towards a cabinet, and Lewis smiled and waved a white hand.

'Help yourself to a drink, my friend. And will you have one, Pellisser?'

'I will,' said Gabriel Pellisser. As Gott filled the glasses, Lewis added:

'I think you can pour another. Manfrey will like one, I'm sure.' He was glancing towards the door, and it opened on his words, for the man-servant to announce:

'Lord Manfrey.'

The third visitor was tall and thin, sparse-haired, and with a small fair moustache.

He blinked about him, and stepped towards the cabinet. He had a high-pitched, grating voice.

"Evening, 'evening. Ah, a drink, I perceive.' He took a bony hand from his pocket, and held it forward. 'This mine—good, good.' He drank quickly. 'Ah—well, Lewis, well? Good news?'

'He's here,' said Gott.

'Ah.' Tension dripped away from Manfrey. 'Excellent work, my dear Lewis, ex-cellent. When I read in an evening paper that he had evaded us, I was positively—ah—afraid.'

Lewis smiled thinly.

'You can't always get your bird with your first barrel, Manfrey.'

'Ah, no. Excellent figure of speech, ah!' He laughed, on a reedy note, and finished his drink. 'May I have one of your ex-cellent cigars, Lewis?' He helped himself from a box on a small table. 'Nothing more to worry about, then, nothing.'

Gott and Pellisser looked towards Lewis.

Nothing in Lewis's expression suggested that he was greatly impressed by his visitors. In fact each would have been aghast had he known Lewis's opinion of him. But whilst Lewis considered all three to be fools of the first order, they had a certain usefulness—albeit that usefulness might end at any moment.

He shrugged.

'I am trying to put the position to you clearly, and without wasting time. Hoppermann is here, and I have little doubt that we can persuade him to do what we want, *but* there are complications. We are not alone in our interest in Hoppermann, gentlemen. The Government—the British Government, I mean—is also interested, and has arranged for some agents to look after our—er—guest. I was at first inclined to under-rate these agents, but on making closer inquiries, since they have worked very quickly and very well indeed, I find that they are members of a Whitehall Department which is very effective. I believe one or more of its members is outside this house now.'

'What?' snapped Pellisser.

'Being watched, you can be assured,' said Lewis. 'The fact that someone was there made me insist that none of you arrive until well after dusk, for recognition would be fatal.' He smiled a little when he saw how the others jumped, then went on: 'It is reasonably certain that these agents know that Hoppermann is here, and they will of course try to get him back.'

'This is ghastly!' exclaimed Manfrey. 'Why did you bring us here? How dare you—'

Lewis snapped: 'I had to consult you, and it had to be here. There are risks in this venture, and you were fully aware of them before we started. Keep quiet, unless you have something constructive to say.'

His voice was not loud, but the tone of it startled the others. Only Gott appeared to be unaffected beyond the first surprise. After a pause he said:

'There's no need for that attitude, Lewis. Manfrey put a reasonable question—if you knew the house was being watched, why did you bring us here?'

'It was necessary,' Lewis began.

'It wasn't. You could have come to see us somewhere else.'

Lewis's lips drew tautly across his teeth.

'We simply don't agree, Gott. I thought it necessary to bring you here, and to tell you exactly what was happening. Do I have to remind you that there are three exits? We can all get away exactly when we want to, and there is no danger provided you keep your heads. I sent for you because we must discuss this together, and we must also get Hoppermann out of the house. It will, of course, be of no further use to us. It is a pity,' he shrugged, 'but one of the inevitable expenses, and after all we are very well paid.' He pressed the tips of his fingers together, then said more crisply: 'We're going to a new house I have obtained in Hampshire. There will be two cars waiting for us on the common at half-past ten, and if necessary we can wait on the common for half-an-hour.' He glanced at a clock above the mantel-shelf, and added unnecessarily, since the others followed his gaze: 'It's now a quarter to ten, and we can get on with some of the business. If there is any approach to the house, we shall be told in good time. Do try to control yourselves.'

Manfrey helped himself to another whisky.

'We have Hoppermann,' Lewis went on, 'and we have a good idea of his purpose here. We want to make sure that he does not get back to America with a report which—'

'I don't like this set-up,' snapped Gott. 'You've got Hoppermann, and we've arranged what is to be done with him. Why the talk?'

Pellisser interjected:

'And there's another thing, Lewis. Why did you bring Hoppermann here? It is a useful rendezvous, and as safe as anywhere in London. Bringing him here has given the police an idea of what's been happening and—'

'Nonsense!' snapped Lewis. 'The police have no such idea. All anyone will know is that Hoppermann was brought here. This house was bought under my name, and I am well known in the district. That will ensure that they will concentrate on looking more for me than any of you.'

Manfrey widened his little eyes.

'Why yes, yes, of course. I didn't understand that, but—very clever of you, Lewis, *ex*-cellent.'

Gott said thinly: 'I don't understand it. We've been here for half-an-hour, and nothing's been said that really matters. Lewis brought us here for some reason he hasn't disclosed, and it looks to me as if he isn't going to disclose it.'

He stopped abruptly.

The door opened, and Lewis rose sharply to his feet, looking at the manservant, who remained sleek and unruffled, but whose dark eyes were excited.

'I think it's time to go, sir.'

'All right, Blake,' said Lewis promptly. 'Gott, we can discuss this later. Have you brought our guest down, Blake?'

'Yes, he's in the passage leading to the common, sir.'

'Good—we'll follow.' Lewis picked up a scarf and wound it round his neck, while Blake helped the visitors into their coats. In a few moments they were all ready. Gott was biting his lips, Manfrey's hands and chin were unsteady, but Lewis was in complete control of himself, and led the way to a narrow passage, at the end of which were two doors. One was standing open, and he stood aside as he reached it.

'There's no hurry,' he said. 'Blake will be at the other end to take you to the cars, they'll be here soon. I—' he paused. 'I must get my case, I've forgotten it.' He waited until all three were hurrying along the passage, Manfrey in the lead, then went back into the lounge. He waited there for two minutes or more, and then he heard a shout from one of the passages.

With a thin-lipped smile, he went to the closed door—not that through which the others had gone—opened it, then hurried through, closing it quickly behind him.

Manfrey, Pellisser and Gott, meanwhile, had reached a narrow flight of steps, just visible in the dim light of the passage. Manfrey stumbled up them, the others muttered as they followed him, and then the cool air of the night swept down on them. Manfrey stumbled again, and then shouted—it was his cry which Lewis had heard.

Gott, the last of the trio, saw vague figures all about him. Someone large and shadowy gripped Manfrey, someone else laid Pellisser low when he tried to evade the shadows. Gott swung round towards the steps, and reached them ahead of either of the men who had selected him—Loftus's men, of course, for Loftus had brought the Department there in force. Gott raced back along the passage when he reached the last step, but at the end he was forced to stop, for the door which had been open was now closed.

He pulled at the handle.

It would not budge. He pushed and pulled, but the door hurt him, being of steel and not of wood. He tried frantically to open it, but despite all his endeavours, the door remained firm. He was still trying when Mike Errol took his arm and led him away. He did not try to fight.

On the common Lewis and Blake, with Hoppermann between them, were hurrying towards a waiting car, two hundred yards from the scene of the scuffle.

1 0

CHASE BY NIGHT

L oftus stood behind a cluster of bushes on the common. Ned Oundle was with him, and a tall man named Carruthers. They could hear the scuffling and an occasional shout from the grounds of Number 4, and Ned said in a deep whisper:

'It looks as if you backed the wrong horse, Bill.'

Loftus smiled, but did not attempt to explain what had persuaded him to wait with the others, and a small cordon of Department men, on the common away from the house.

To him, the arrival of Hoppermann by taxi at Number 4 seemed to cry suspicion aloud. The abductors must have known that Hoppermann had been followed. Taking him to a house which, in all likelihood, would be immediately covered by the Department or the police, would be a fool's trick.

These men were not fools!

So, he reasoned, Hoppermann had been taken to the house deliberately, *to get Department men there.*

It was reasonable to presume that the instigators of the

crime would not invite arrest, and the obvious ruse was to get away from the house by a means not generally known. The house was near enough to the common for a passage to be tunnelled to another exit. The passage could not be too long, and, as far as he could see, this cluster of bushes was the nearest point to the house which, if there was a hidden exit, could provide reasonable cover by day. The people who had prepared the exit, if there was one, could not be sure that they would have to use it by day.

Consequently he had placed a small cordon about the bushes, and with Ned and Carruthers was waiting there himself. The sounds from the house suggested that some of the occupants had been caught, but that was by no means proof that all of them were in the Department's hands.

There were several minutes of utter silence. They seemed much longer than they were, and Loftus was beginning to give up hope, when he heard a creaking noise not far away, and then a dull thud.

He stiffened, and his hand went to his pocket.

Then he heard another creak, followed by the sound of heavy breathing. It was too dark to see anything clearly, but suddenly Loftus was able to discern the silhouettes of two or three men at the far end of the bushes. He stepped softly towards them, with the others on his heels, and then Ned Oundle caught his foot on a tree-root, and stumbled.

Loftus heard a curse.

He snatched out his gun, but as he did so he felt rather than saw a movement. He did not see anything coming through the air towards him, but he did hear a slight tinkle, and he shouted:

'*Get away!*'

He leapt to one side, but swiftly though he moved, his eyes

were beginning to water, and he felt a sharp acridness at his mouth and nose. He recognised tear-gas, and was relieved that nothing more deadly had been released. As he went out of the immediate range of the gas he was thinking that his adversaries were prepared for every emergency.

He hoped he was equally prepared.

He took a match-box from his pocket, but the matches therein were not of the ordinary kind. He struck one, and tossed it away from him. It gave out a surprisingly bright, lurid light, which illuminated an area of some seventy square feet.

In the glow he saw the outlines of a car, fifty feet or so away from him, and three men running towards it. He recognised Hoppermann's tall figure between two other men. He saw Hoppermann stop suddenly, heard an oath, saw the stab of flame from an automatic which one of the others carried.

Hoppermann fell.

The others kept on. The engine of the car started up, and the car moved as the men swung open the doors and threw themselves inside. Loftus shouted:

'Look after Hoppermann!'

His own car was parked not thirty yards away, and he raced towards it. The glow of light was fading, but it was still enough for him to see by. Ned Oundle was gasping by the bushes, Carruthers was staggering further away, with a handkerchief to his eyes and mouth. But other Department men out of range of the tear-gas, were hot foot after the car.

It sped along the common.

Loftus reached his own, started the engine, and turned swiftly in pursuit. The match still showed a faint light, revealing the dark shape of his quarry over a hundred yards away; there was no rear-light.

Loftus switched on his head-lamps.

The light caught the red reflector of the car ahead, enabling him to keep it in sight. It turned on the road leading to Putney Hill, and then after five minutes started up the rise. There was little traffic, although as he swung round a corner, Loftus saw a cyclist loom up, and could even see the terrified expression on the rider's face.

He turned his wheel sharply.

He avoided the cyclist by inches, then went roaring up the hill, getting to the top in time to see that the other car now had its lights on, and had turned right, towards Roehampton Village.

He began to toy with the idea of switching off his lights, and when they were past the village and on the Kingston by-pass, he did so, on a curve which would make it impossible for the occupants of the first car to see what he had done. When he swung round the bend, he saw the red rear-light glowing, and after a few seconds the pace of the other car slowed down.

It did so abruptly, and he had to brake quickly after finding the car looming in front of him, a silhouette against its own head-lights. Loftus tightened his lips and his heart beat fast, but soon he was over that emergency, and following the other car at a distance of some thirty yards.

Mile after mile he followed it, wondering, when at last he reached the Basingstoke-London road, near Hook, whether he had enough petrol in his tank to take him on the full length of the journey.

At Basingstoke the leading car took the Winchester Road. Some five miles along it, it disappeared.

Loftus jammed on his brakes.

They squealed protestingly, and the Jaguar lurched to a standstill. Loftus sat forward, crouching a little, expecting something to come out of the darkness. His heart was thumping, and there was a beading of sweat on his forehead. But he heard nothing, and he could see nothing; the pitch-blackness of the night was about him like a shroud.

He eased the car towards the side of the road, and then pulled up again.

He was swearing under his breath as he lit a cigarette, cupping the flare of the match in his hands to prevent it from showing far. He realised that he had probably been seen, that the leader must have turned off his lights and gone on.

He waited for five minutes, then switched on rear and side-lights. Then he climbed out of the car. It was surprisingly cold, but windless.

He walked up and down for some seconds, getting himself warmer, trying to work out the best thing to do.

Could the car have disappeared completely?

He walked on a little further, then discovered a sharp turn to the left.

Loftus frowned.

'That's probably it,' he said. 'It went down here.'

He waited again, silently, his figure hidden by the darkness. He was quite sure that no one else was nearby; even the creatures of the night appeared to have been forced to silence. He shone his torch, reading the names of several houses. *The Beeches, Conway, Fern Hill*—he found seven in all. In which had his quarry taken refuge?

He switched off his torch, and kept quite still. Then to his straining ears there came the sound of stealthy footsteps somewhere nearby. Eventually they drew nearer, and he was able to locate them. He stepped slowly forward, gun in hand.

At a distance of no more than five feet he saw a man.

He saw, also, that the man appeared to be peering about

him. Loftus waited for another second, while the other took two further steps forward, then said in a low voice:

'Keep quite still.'

Whoever it was had a steady nerve. The man stopped, but uttered no sound, no gasp of surprise, of fear. The silence continued until Loftus said:

'Put your hands up high.'

The man obeyed. Loftus frisked him, and took a gun from his hip-pocket. He could hear the man's heavy breathing, then heard the other speak in a voice as low pitched as his own.

'Dunster,' came the voice. 'R-E-T—'

Loftus felt an immense wave of relief, and grinned widely.

'Dunster, bless your heart!' The reverse spelling removed all possible doubt of the identity of the other man. Dunster, who at Mike's behest had followed the cab in which Christine Weston had been taken on from Putney.

Thought of Hoppermann's daughter, and the presence of Dunster, brought queries tumbling over one another, but he forced himself to think of the present, to worry about developments and theories afterwards.

Dunster sounded overjoyed.

'I tried the spelling as a forlorn hope—Bill, you idiot, you had me scared!'

'You didn't show it,' said Loftus. 'How long have you been here?'

'It seems like a couple of nights and days,' said Dunster, 'but it can't be more than three hours. I couldn't get away to a 'phone, and I thought I'd better hang around until morning, or until something turned up.'

'Good man. You followed the cab and the girl? Did you see what house they went in?'

'Yes,' said Dunster. 'It's a new place, called *Conway*, I nearly lost them several times. This little turning put me off, but there's a straight stretch ahead, and I knew the cab couldn't have got out of sight, so I came back. I saw them going into a house—*Conway*, as I say. The second driveway on the right. They carried the girl in. She looked ghastly—the moon was shining on her, and her face was like wax. She—but it's no time for talking. What are you going to do?'

Loftus pursed his lips.

'I think we'd better do it this way,' he said. 'Get to a telephone—knock up a pub, or a private house if needs be —'phone Craigie, and ask him to send the Errols, Carruthers, and several of the others here. Give precise instructions, and get some local people to tell you how to approach from the rear of the house, so that it's well covered, and then come back and keep your eyes open.'

'What are you going to do?'

'I'll be inside *Conway*,' said Loftus quietly.

'In—' Dunster's voice sounded very loud. 'Don't be a fool, Bill, they'll cut your throat as soon as look at you.'

Loftus chuckled softly.

We'll try to avoid it. Don't let yourself get caught, and if anyone leaves, follow them. Where's your car?'

'Parked down the road—there's a wide grass verge.'

'Good man. You might put mine there. I—no, I think we'll leave mine where it is,' said Loftus. We don't want to start an engine here, and you can walk to the 'phone. Tell Craigie just what I'm doing, and also that I am allowing myself to be taken.'

'Look here, it sounds pretty dumb to me,' said Dunster dubiously. 'If you wait for me to get back, we could have a shot at it together. We might do something then.'

Loftus rested a hand on his shoulder.

'Don't worry, old son, more is won by acting like a fool than you might think. I'll get in, you finish your job with

Craigie and then be ready to follow anyone who comes out. Right?'

'Right,' said Dunster, dubiously.

He went off, moving quietly into the darkness.

Loftus found the gate marked 'Conway', and turned down the gravel drive, shining his torch until he could just see the house in the far extremity of the beam. He switched off, and stepped to the grass verge bordering the drive.

He went forward very slowly, threading his way through a shrubbery, and hearing every time he paused, a stealthy movement not far away from him. It was weird to be moving there, sure that he was being watched, knowing that his watcher might decide to shoot first and ask questions afterwards.

Then he heard another, louder movement just behind him, and a voice sounded just as his had sounded when he had spoken to Dunster.

'Keep quite still!'

Loftus went rigid. The voice was rough, and carried a note of menace. He felt a hand touch his shoulder, then a man gripped his right arm, twisting it quickly in a half-Nelson, which made him gasp involuntarily. His gun fell to the grass.

He was frisked quickly and expertly.

There were two men behind him, and although the pressure on his arm relaxed they did not take the chance of letting him go.

'Okay,' growled one of them. 'You git on.'

The order was helped by a knee to the buttocks, but Loftus was less concerned with the attitude of these rough-necks than with what would happen when he was taken into the house.

He wondered whether Lewis would be there.

He wondered whether Christine Weston was hurt.

And above all he wondered why it had been thought necessary to recapture her. Had she told him the truth? Did she know more than she said? Or was it possible that she had some knowledge of an importance which was unknown to her?

He was thinking of all those things as he was taken to the door of *Conway,* and hustled inside.

11

LOFTUS V. LEWIS

The bright light of the small, square hall in which he found himself dazzled him, so that he closed his eyes and waited for some seconds before opening them. The waiting was accompanied by another knee to his buttocks, and he had to clench his teeth to prevent himself from a retaliatory move which might yield disastrous results.

But when he was able to look about him, he turned on his heel. very quickly, making the men behind him raise their guns. As men go, they were not small; but Loftus towered above them. Their faces were set in an expression which showed a hard-bitten toughness; but this toughness did not out-do the toughness of Bill Loftus.

'If that happens again,' he said, 'there is going to be a broken neck.'

The man who had kneed him was a yard behind him, blunt-faced, menacing. He opened his lips to snap a retort, but the words were not uttered. He stared at Loftus for perhaps ten seconds, then evaded his eyes.

'Git on,' he said.

'Supposing one of you leads the way?' said Loftus.

It was absurd; he might have been giving orders instead of subjected to them, with two armed men present to reinforce any command. But it worked, for one of the men grunted and pushed past him towards a narrow passage. His broad shoulders nearly touched it, and Loftus brushed against it on both sides. Why a passage should be so skimped he did not know, but it widened after a couple of yards, and the leading man unlatched a door.

This opened to another passage, leading in turn to the front hall. There, without ostentation, was affluence. It showed in the highly polished floors, the Persian rugs, the rich velvet curtains. Loftus looked about him as the first man turned up a wide shallow staircase, with a wrought-iron balustrade.

From the landing led two corridors. The first was short and leading to another flight of stairs, the second wide, with windows on one side, and four doors on the other. The windows were heavily curtained. Loftus was reflecting that the lay-out of the house was unusual and storing up all details for possible exploration later, when the leader tapped on the second door.

There was a pause, and then:

'What is it?'

Loftus waited with keen interest, and was certain of one thing; the rough-neck was nervous. It gave Loftus an impression of the character of the man he was to meet, for neither rough-neck impressed him as being likely to be easily cowed into tame submission.

Even the gruff voice was meek.

'We gotta guy in the grounds, Boss.'

Loftus was wondering whether the American accent was natural or assumed, but had no time to wonder long, for the door opened to reveal a short, thin man, dark, well-dressed, good-looking yet not attractive. His hair was too long, his coat too waisted, his eyes too large and brilliant. Loftus did not think it was the man whose voice he had first heard, and he was right, for this apparition spoke in a faintly supercilious and lilting voice, with a faintly foreign accent.

'Bring him in, Stocker.'

Stocker was the leader, and he stood aside for Loftus to enter, his gun much in evidence. The other thug followed Loftus into a large, square room, pleasantly furnished and creating an air of affluence similar to that of the hall.

It was neither lounge nor study, but an admirable compromise. At one end of the room were three large leather easy chairs with velvet cushions, and a long, low divan—at the other was a desk and two filing cabinets.

A man was sitting at the desk.

He was tall; that Loftus judged from his broad shoulders and his height above the desk. His face was tanned, suggesting perfect health, his eyes were dark, the whites very clear. He had full, sensitive lips, and he looked faintly amused.

'You've caught quite a big fish, Stocker.'

Loftus was eyeing him evenly, but with eyes half-narrowed.

'I think—' the man at the desk went on, but Loftus interrupted him, taking a leap in the dark. Lewis was the owner of 4 Lester Drive, and it was possible that this man was Lewis.

'Mr. Lewis, I presume,' he said almost casually, and, while the other's expression gave him away: 'Do you mind if I smoke?'

Without waiting for a reply he stepped forward and took a cigarette from an open box on the desk, putting it to his lips. The move had taken him two yards nearer Lewis, but he did not look at the man. His eyes roved for matches, and he saw a box at the other end of the desk. He stretched out and picked it up.

Then Stocker hit him.

Loftus was half-prepared for it, or the blow would have unsteadied him. It was aimed at his lips, and was probably intended to crush the cigarette against his mouth. He moved his head sideways, and the blow just caught his shoulders. He saw that Stocker was momentarily off his balance, and hit the man with all the power there was in him.

He had little room for a swing, and the punch was no more than a short-arm jab, but it moved with such speed and precision that Stocker crashed back against a chair, and then sprawled over it.

Loftus struck a match and lit his cigarette.

For a few seconds the silence in the room was absolute. Then Lewis began to drum his fingers lightly on his desk. The man who had been with Stocker moved forward and hoisted his companion to a sitting position. Stocker had the dazed expression of a man knocked flat out; his teeth were clenched tightly, his eyelids were fluttering.

'Is this man armed, Jackson?' said Lewis.

'We took his gun,' said the second rough-neck.

'Leave Stocker, and make sure,' said Lewis.

He had opened a drawer in his desk, and as he spoke he put a small automatic in front of him. He waited while Jackson frisked Loftus again, satisfying himself that he had no weapons.

'He's clean, boss.'

'Then take Stocker away, and be ready to come up here when I ring for you,' said Lewis.

He watched Jackson pull Stocker from the chair, and support him to the door. Stocker's legs would not do what he told them, and he was muttering to himself. The long-haired man stepped to the door and opened it, and the rough-necks went into the passage. When the door closed, Lewis said:

'Stay by the door, Pierre.'

The long-haired man obeyed. Loftus was conscious of the fact that his too-large, too-bright eyes were boring into his back, but he kept his own gaze firmly on Lewis, who said at last:

'That was a prodigious feat of strength.'

'Yes, wasn't it?' said Loftus. He drew easily at his cigarette, and added: 'We may as well complete the introductions. My name is Loftus.'

He wanted to see the effect of that bold statement, and he had considerable satisfaction. Lewis was not a man likely to show his emotions easily, but his lips parted and his eyes widened. Moreover, his right hand moved towards the gun in front of him.

'How did you get here?'

'I followed you from Putney,' said Loftus.

'That is untrue. No one followed me.'

'Wrong in one,' said Loftus. 'You missed me near Roehampton, but I'd only switched off the lights. Not a pleasant drive, but an effective one.'

'I see. Ingenious as well as powerful.'

'Oh, a little of everything,' said Loftus airily.

'How did you get to Lester Drive?'

'Come, come. You invited me there. You had Hoppermann taken there, and you arranged for others to visit you at the house—I've been watching it for some time, and the reports I've had are very comprehensive.'

There was a moment of silence before Lewis stood up. He held the gun in his hand.

'What made you think that I expected you to go to Lester Drive?'

'Because I knew you weren't likely to be so careless as the move appeared,' said Loftus.

'I don't know why you think you are in no great danger, but obviously you aren't perturbed. How soon do you expect help?'

'Oh, just about in time, I think,' said Loftus.

'You're wrong,' said Lewis. 'Whenever it comes it will be too late.' He spoke firmly, but Loftus sensed uncertainty in him, knew that Lewis was wondering *why* the captive seemed so sure of himself.

'Too late, too late,' he said briskly. 'That's a parrot-cry I've heard so often that it gets tiring. Lewis, it's time we talked seriously, and stopped this fencing.' He paused for a moment, and his eyes were very direct. Despite the quickness of his ensuing words he chose them carefully, anxious not to say one too many or too few. 'I propose to find out why you want Hoppermann dead, I propose also to find what part you are playing in the peculiar business of United States help. The general impression is that you, with others, are a foreign agent, but I am inclined to doubt it.'

Lewis spoke a shade too quickly.

'Why?'

'I think I'll keep my reasons to myself,' said Loftus. 'You might think they're half-baked.' He grinned suddenly, almost boyishly. 'I propose to find your motivation, and to find out who is helping you. The tie-up is between someone this side, and someone in the States, of course. It may seem a tall order, but the Department has tackled worse. The Department,' he added carefully, 'is a thing on which you should ponder carefully. There are a lot of agents, and I'm just one of them. The only difference is in our names. We have a record of which we're absurdly proud—*we haven't failed yet.*'

A slight pause before the 'we' gave emphasis to the final

sentence, as he intended. He saw Lewis's eyes narrow, and he believed that he had made a second step towards undermining the man's confidence.

'There is plenty of time,' said Lewis.

'There is indeed. We have all the time in the world, *and* all the resources. You can't beat us, Lewis. Your only chance would have been had you, or anyone else, been able to work, without discovery, until your plans were so near fruition that nothing could stop them. That hasn't happened. I'll repeat—*you can't beat us.* From midnight to-night, unless you have been apprehended earlier, a house-to-house search has been instituted by the police, just for you. There are to be no half measures, but—' he paused, wondering how Lewis was taking this, wondering also whether the gigantic bluff he was trying would work. He wanted one thing: *time*, time for the others to get here.

'But what?' Lewis gave nothing away.

Loftus shrugged. 'It seems to me that you can ensure your personal safety by the complete confession, implicating all those working with you, and stating fully the motive of your actions against Hoppermann. How does that strike you as a proposition?'

12

THE CONFIDENCE OF LEWIS

L oftus stepped towards an easy chair, and sat on the arm.
It was so well-sprung that he swayed back a little; and
then, for the first time, Pierre spoke.

'Keep very still, Loftus.' His accent was French, and Loftus,
who could see him out of the corner of his eye, saw that he too
held a gun. He ignored Pierre completely.

Lewis's fingers were drumming.

'Are you serious with your proposition, Loftus?'

'Quite serious.'

'Have you authority for it?'

'Yes,' said Loftus promptly, and for the first time it passed
through his mind that the bluff might work.

'Whose authority?'

'I think you'll just have to take my word that it's good
enough,' Loftus said.

'That is hardly sufficient, Loftus. In fact I am inclined to
think that you invented that proposition on the spur of the
moment, to—could it be to gain time?'

'Yes, of course, it could! It's quite an idea.' Loftus lifted a hand, palm outwards. 'That's the trouble with having a tortuous mind, Lewis. When a straight offer is made it is viewed with suspicion. However, there is the offer. I'll say again, *you* can't succeed. True, you might cause serious dissensions between good friends, but in the end, sense will prevail and you may find yourself imprisoned for life. Not a nice prospect.'

Lewis drummed his fingers even harder. 'I know the risks. You under-rate my preparedness, Loftus. You made an interesting proviso just now. You suggested that the one way in which any organisation could beat your Department was by being almost finished before anything was discovered. I *am* so prepared. The matter is in its final stages. In fact the final stages will be reached abroad, not here. There is nothing you can do to stop me.'

'Then you must be mad,' said Loftus blandly. 'And somehow I don't think that you are. Come, Lewis, your anxiety to get Hoppermann isn't without cause. Unless he could smash your plans, you'd leave him alone.'

Both Pierre and Lewis kept very still, and Loftus felt he had succeeded in breaking through their complacency. What was more, he had gained another twenty minutes at least; nearly an hour-and-a-half had passed since Dunster had gone to telephone.

'Your imagination does you credit,' sneered Lewis. 'Hoppermann can possibly create a trifling delay—'

'Again, that's just too bad,' said Loftus blandly. 'And his daughter, of course.'

He saw Lewis's teeth bare, heard a sudden oath from Pierre. All at once he was aware that both men were much more dangerous, that the tension which had relaxed a little was back to its limit.

Because of mention of Christine.

Lewis kept his temper with an obvious effort.

'Stocker was right,' he said. 'You talk far too freely, Loftus. I'm tired of talking to you. You have no chance at all of succeeding, and your wonderful friends'—he sneered the word—'will be as foolish as you if they try to interfere. I will spend ten minutes in showing you, also, that I am in no personal danger.'

He turned to the wall, and pressed a button; a section of the wall opened, revealing a mirror and a dressing-table, or something like it, built into the wall. He sat down opposite the mirror, opened a drawer and took out a box, of the square, flat kind containing theatrical make-up.

Loftus knew the value of disguise, although he did not indulge in it himself. He realised, as he watched, that Lewis was going to make a flamboyant gesture to show the reason for his confidence—but in the next five minutes he was appalled.

Lewis was already disguised!

The handsome tanned complexion disappeared under the touch of a cleansing cream. The well-marked eyebrows were combed and brushed out, the sleek hair was powdered and rubbed briskly. It was all done very quickly—and although Loftus was actually watching the metamorphosis, he could not really believe it.

Lewis was perhaps ten minutes in front of the mirror. When he had finished he seemed a much older man, his complexion pasty, even raddled. He said sharply:

'Watch him, Pierre.'

Pierre made a single comment, and Lewis pulled at a knob in the wall, so that it opened into a six-feet-high screen, self-coloured with the wall. There was a rattle of metal on metal, a rustling, and occasionally the top of Lewis's now fluffy hair showed above the screen; his feet were visible all the time.

Loftus sat quite still, lit a third cigarette, and glanced covertly at his watch.

An hour and forty minutes had gone.

Then the screen was folded back into the wall, and Lewis stepped into the full light of the room.

Loftus stared.

He saw a tall, stout man, badly dressed, with sloping shoulders and sagging stomach. Gone was the exquisitely-cut suit, upright carriage, the lean, healthy figure. This was a stranger. He moved in a slow, ungainly fashion towards the desk, very different from his earlier lithe, graceful movements.

The explanation was simple, of course; too simple.

This *was* the man.

The other was a carefully-assumed disguise, effective because of its apparent naturalness and because there had been no reason to believe it was anything but the man's real appearance. But this was Lewis, a big, untidy, rather dirty-looking man, with pasty face and muddy-coloured whites to his eyes—achieved, no doubt, by drops just inserted—who would never be recognised as the man from Lester Drive.

Lewis spoke; and the change in his voice was just as definite: his accent was now guttural, faintly Central European.

'You are now one of the very few men, Loftus, who has seen me as both myself *and* Lewis. I expect that your friends will soon be here—that is why you talked, I know. But what will they see? *Me.* Not Lewis. *Me!* I am a most harmless old man, Loftus, and am well-liked. But the drive to *Conway* also leads—though few know it—to the house next door. A house which will explode—and very soon, now—just like the house in Barnes. A man like Lewis has often been seen there. I will say so, Pierre will say so, my servants will say so. You understand? A clever scheme, is it not?'

Loftus said: 'It's clever, yes.'

'It is perfect,' said Lewis. He stepped to the desk, and his finger touched a bell-push. He went on: 'That is for Stocker and Jackson, or if Stocker is not well enough, another. You will be taken next door. Mrs Weston will go also. The two of you, so soon to die.'

'Why the girl?' Loftus asked casually.

'Because she makes a nuisance of herself,' said Lewis viciously, his previous buoyancy changing to sudden ill-temper. 'She always makes trouble.'

Loftus picked up yet another cigarette, and fumbled in the match-box for a match. His hands seemed unsteady, and the cigarette trembled a little between his lips. Before he could speak, there was a tap on the door.

'Come in,' said Lewis.

But he spoke from the wall, and he had hidden himself behind the screen; his voice was the voice Loftus had first heard.

The door opened, and Jackson came through, with the sleek servant—Blake of Lester Drive, although Loftus did not know that.

Lewis spoke from behind the screen.

'Take this man next door. And the woman.'

The economy of words suggested to Loftus that Lewis was still out of temper, and he could not understand why, after a period of utter calmness and the show of such self-confidence, mention of Christine Weston should make such a difference.

He had let his cigarette go out deliberately, and as the two men approached, warily, for Jackson would not easily forget what had happened to Stocker, he took a match from the box. This time his fingers did not fumble, he said lightly:

'A last cigarette, I hope.'

Then he struck the match.

It did what had seemed impossible a split-second before. It

rooted Jackson and Blake to the floor, it made Lewis exclaim in alarm, it brought another vicious French oath from Pierre. Pierre fired towards Loftus, but the bullet missed.

The match was similar to the one he had used at Putney.

Loftus flung it from him as soon as it started to burn, and then, his eyes closed against the glare, he moved for the door. He struck against either Jackson or Blake, he did not know which, and sent in a jab which took the man in the stomach. The dull thud of the blow, and the hollow gasp which followed, merged with the echoes of Pierre's shot.

Loftus reached the door.

The brightness of the light was undimmed, and he knew it would be some minutes before any of them could focus their eyes properly. To improve his chances he struck another match and flung it towards Pierre, then groped for and found the handle of the door. He pushed it to behind him, for it opened outwards into the passage, then looked hastily up and down. The furniture in the passage was vague and blurred, but what looked like a long, wooden blanket box was not far away. He reached it, and was able to lift it, although with a considerable effort.

He put it down, with a thud, swinging it round so that it stood lengthwise from the door, with something like a couple of feet between the end of the box and the opposite wall. Another glance about him not only showed him a heavy wooden chair, but proved that his vision was much better. He moved, and it just fitted into the gap, so that anyone trying to shift the door would find it immovable.

Then he tried the doors along the passage. None was locked, and all the rooms were empty. He retraced his footsteps, and he was glad to hear a thudding noise against the blocked door; it suggested that there was no other exit. But he did not let himself be too sanguine; Lewis could be crafty enough to have the noise made to cover movements in another direction.

Crossing the landing, Loftus tried the doors in the passage leading to the second flight of stairs. The thudding increased, and was only half-drowned by the noise of Loftus putting a shoulder to a door which was locked.

He was wondering, then, whether there were other men in the house besides Stocker.

This door was a much stiffer problem than those at Barnes, and his shoulder was aching from the effort. But at last he heard a splintering of wood, and the door crashed open.

He just prevented himself from falling into the room.

It was a bedroom, and pleasantly-furnished, although he saw that only subconsciously. He had eyes only for the girl.

The last time he had found her she had been tied to a camp bed, but was conscious. This time she was lying, fully clad and in the frock which she had borrowed from Diana's flat; sight of it again made him tighten his lips. She was neither gagged nor bound; but she lay limp and apparently lifeless, and he remembered Dunster's words about her pallor.

He went forward, and lifted her from the bed, then turned back to the door, acutely conscious of the danger which still confronted him. He would have felt ten times safer with a gun, but there had been no time to get one in Lewis's room; time spent groping for it might have proved fatal.

The passage was empty.

He reached the head of the stairs, and the thudding against the other door increased, grew frenzied. There was a louder, sharper note, suggesting that something hard was being used as a battering ram. The fact that no one else had appeared suggested the house was otherwise empty—Stocker always excepted.

He hurried down the stairs.

He did nothing to try to muffle his footsteps; caution and speed would not go together, and the first essential was certainly speed. But to a degree at least that proved a mistake, for as he reached the foot of the stairs he saw a leg shoot out, level with the bottom step. He had no time to evade it. He went sprawling, and he had all his work cut out to prevent Christine's head thudding against the floor. He banged his own head, but lightly, and when he was able to see past Christine, he saw Stocker.

The man's eyes were glittering viciously. He had a gun, butt foremost, in his hand, and he was no more than two yards away. Loftus was on his back, the girl lying across him. Stocker kicked at his waist, making him grunt, but Loftus put up a hand and forced the man's wrist away as it began to descend for the first blow.

Stocker drew back, and hesitated. Perhaps he was naturally slow-witted, perhaps the earlier blow still affected him. At all events, he paused, standing within reach of Loftus's foot, and Loftus hooked his legs from under him.

Stocker fell heavily.

Loftus pushed the girl aside, and struggled up. There was desperation in his mind—he must finish Stocker for the time being. The man was trying to get at the gun, which had fallen from his grasp, but Loftus pushed him aside, stooped down and picked up the automatic.

As he reached it Stocker got to his feet, kicked again at Loftus, and gained a momentary respite. Had the man decided to stay and fight, Loftus doubted whether he could have won through, but Stocker took to his heels, pushing open a door leading, presumably, to the kitchen quarters. The door swung behind him, while Loftus brushed his hair back from his forehead and, retaining a grip on the gun, lifted the girl and slung her, fireman-fashion, over his left shoulder.

He pulled aside the curtains at the front door. It was bolted, and he drew the bolts, then slid back the latch. Gun poking forward, he reached the porch.

As he stepped outside it he saw something strike at his outstretched hand—then felt excruciating pain in his wrist, forcing him to let the gun drop. As it fell, he saw Lewis—the real, the second Lewis—and Pierre, on either side of the porch.

Pierre retained his gun.

13
DEVELOPMENTS OF IMPORTANCE

L oftus stood quite still, with the girl over his shoulder. His own shadow was thrown clearly to the drive immediately outside the front door, and that of the girl made him look hunched and mis-shapen. The light streamed into the grounds.

His wrist was numb, and he knew it was quite useless to try to get away. He had learned enough of Pierre and Lewis to be sure that they would not take kindly to the earlier rebuff; their thoughts would turn immediately to revenge in kind.

He waited for the bullet.

It did not come.

Lewis spoke very softly. 'Turn round, Loftus.'

Loftus half-turned.

Then, from somewhere in the grounds, there came a high-pitched cry. It had the eeriness of an owl's call, sudden and sharp and uttered three times, then fading into the silence and the darkness. It made Pierre start and turn sharply, while Lewis said:

'Hurry, damn you!'

Loftus quickened his pace, but kicked against the step leading into the hall, and stumbled. As he did so he heard a gasp from Pierre, then the sharp sneezing sound of the Frenchman's effectively silenced automatic. He heard movements in the grounds, and straightened up, getting into the hall although handicapped by the girl.

Lewis moved past him.

Just for that moment Loftus thought that it was the end, for Lewis also had an automatic, and although he was moving fast he delayed long enough to turn and point the gun towards him. Loftus did the only thing he could; he sat down abruptly, letting the girl fall with him. The bullet went over his head, while the sounds of movement outside increased, and Lewis turned, racing towards the kitchen quarters.

Pierre was backing into the house, firing from time to time. Whatever his looks, the man was no coward. Loftus could see moving figures on the drive, and knew—as he had known when the call had first come—that Department men were in the grounds.

Pierre, still backing, reached the hall. The yellow flame from his gun was almost lost in the bright hall light. Loftus, still in a sitting position, hitched himself forward and pushed a leg out, so that Pierre struck against it and stumbled. Trip-ups, thought Loftus, were two-a-penny.

The sight of Pierre stumbling brought two of Craigie's men into the hall at the double; clearly they had been waiting for that chance, as clearly they had not used their guns for fear of hitting Loftus. Reaching Pierre before the man could recover his balance, they wrenched the gun from his hand.

Loftus stood up.

Mike and Mark Errol, Dunster and Carruthers, were crowding into the hall. Dunster was the first to speak.

'We managed it, Bill. Are you sitting pretty?'

Loftus smiled.

'I was. There's a big fellow gone towards the kitchen—are the side and back doors being watched?'

'Yes,' said Mike and Mark Errol simultaneously.

'Good work,' said Loftus. 'How many men have we on the premises?'

'A dozen,' said Ned Oundle from the open door.

He came into the hall, and after satisfying himself that Loftus was not badly hurt, turned towards the girl. He frowned, and bent down near her. Loftus was gently massaging his wrist while giving instructions. Three other Department men had followed Ned into the hall; the rest were watching the side and back doors, and the drive gates.

Loftus led the way upstairs.

The banging had stopped, but when he opened the door which he had blocked half-an-hour before, he found Blake and Jackson by the wall. Neither showed any signs of making a struggle, and it was not long before they were talking viciously of Lewis who, with Pierre, had gone out of a door in the wall, next to the screen and mirror, promising to leave the passage free, but locking the door behind them.

Loftus heard the story, and shrugged his shoulders.

'Lewis is a mile ahead of any double-crosser I've met,' he said.

He paid little attention to Blake and Jackson, who were hustled downstairs, but continued the search of the house. All he discovered, in the course of the next hour, was that every-thing which might conceivably harbour letters or papers appeared to be empty.

There was no sign of Lewis.

No one had seen him, and no one—except perhaps Pierre —knew of any other exit from the house. That there was one Loftus did not doubt.

Pierre maintained a tight-lipped silence.

Loftus spent little time talking to him. He wanted to complete a thorough search of the house, and of the place 'next door'. That proved to be a smaller property, and the man-servant Blake talked freely about it. It had been rented furnished, and there were times when Lewis had a dozen or more men staying there, all of the Stocker and Jackson variety.

That was not surprising.

Blake, moreover, knew that a charge of nitroglycerine was deposited in the cellar of the rented house, and could be fired at any given time by electric control from *Conway.* After the charges had been discovered, and removed with great care, the second house was searched as thoroughly as the first, but the results were no more encouraging. There was, however, plenty of evidence of occupation. One room had been turned into a clubroom; there were two small billiard-tables, dart boards, cards, dominoes, chess—a diversity of games, in fact which suggested that Lewis had taken great trouble to make sure that the men he commanded were not bored.

But of documents there was none.

In three of the bedrooms at the smaller house, however, the book-cases were illuminating. There were illustrated magazines from Eastern Germany; and there were three- and four-week-old Russian newspapers.

Ned Oundle and the Errols accompanied Loftus on his search. Dunster and one of the other men were looking after Christine Weston, although it was clear that she was likely to remain unconscious for some time. The transparent whiteness of her complexion was disturbing, but there was nothing Loftus could do immediately, although he arranged for her to be taken with the first car-load of Department men.

Local police were summoned and, at four o'clock in the morning, Loftus, the Errols and Ned Oundle climbed into a second car, a third car-load starting after them. Three Department men were left at the house, but the local police were now in charge.

Blake, Jackson and Stocker were also taken over by the police, but Pierre was in the car with Loftus. For safety's sake the man was bound at the wrists. He sat in a corner, saying nothing, refusing a cigarette when offered one.

Pierre, thought Loftus, would certainly not be persuaded to talk by normal means, and certainly not by measures which the police would approve.

After an uneventful journey, the others, except Ned Oundle, piled out of the car in Brook Street, taking Pierre with them to Loftus's flat. Loftus and Ned, with Ned driving, went to Whitehall, but there was no response to a ring at Craigie's office. Loftus was one of the few men who could get into the office when it was unoccupied, but there was no one inside when he did step through.

There was, however, a note on the desk. Craigie had written cryptically:

Come to Number 10.

Oundle widened his eyes.

'Hallo, hallo! Developments of importance, it seems.'

'It could be,' said Loftus. 'What happened at Lester Drive, precisely?'

'I don't know,' said Oundle. 'Three of the blokes were caught, but who they were Craigie didn't vouchsafe. We ransacked the house, but didn't find anything of importance, and we were still working there when Craigie 'phoned us to get after you.'

'H-mm,' said Loftus thoughtfully. 'Well, I'd better go over to No. 10. Are you coming?'

'I am not,' said Oundle decisively. He had a horror, none knew why, of being interviewed by celebrities, and had been known to declare that Cabinet Ministers were the only people in the world who could scare him. Knowing that trait in his character, Loftus did not try persuasion.

Oundle was lucky in finding a night duty taxi to take him to Brook Street, while Loftus, after much trouble with the police and sentries on duty, was ushered into Number 10.

It was not his first visit to that house of tradition, but he always felt an odd sense of quiet when he stepped over the threshold. Usually, that went immediately he saw Hershall, and it was so again.

The Prime Minister was in a small study, and Craigie was sitting in an easy chair. Hershall stood with his back to an electric fire, for the night was chilly. He had a dark blue silk dressing-gown wrapped tightly about him, and the first impression Loftus had of him was a man in a monk's habit, for the hunched shoulders made the dressing-gown droop from him, almost to the floor.

A cheroot poked characteristically from the Premier's mouth.

As well as Hershall and Craigie there were two other men in the room. Loftus recognized them both. One was Whitterly, the head of Intelligence, of which Department Z was a small but autonomous branch.

A man of medium height, square-shouldered, brisk speaking and brisk moving. Lt.-Colonel Bruce Whitterly had been a fine soldier, and made a good job of his present appointment.

The fourth man was the Rt. Hon. Jonathan Scott, the Foreign Secretary, short, bulky, aggressive. Both he and Whitterly, although fully-dressed, were unshaven.

The door closed behind Loftus.

Hershall took the cheroot from his lips and said abruptly:

'We've been waiting for you.'

Loftus smiled. 'I'm sorry I'm late, but things have been somewhat hectic.' He put a small attaché case on the table, one which contained the magazines and the newspapers found in the house next door to *Conway*, then made a quick statement of what had happened.

When he had finished, Scott said:

'Pity you went in, Loftus. If you'd waited outside you could have caught this fellow, what's-his-name.'

Loftus shrugged. 'It's just possible. But I wanted to try to make sure that Hoppermann's daughter was safe.'

Craigie uncrossed his thin legs.

'The men arrested at the Putney house, Bill, were Lord Manfrey, Sir Geoffrey Gott, and Gabriel Pellisser. None of them was ever suspected of Communist or Fascist sympathies, but all have admitted to conspiracy against the State. They make it clear—' Craigie's voice was very dry and crisp, he might have been discussing some triviality—'that there is a widespread subversive organisation in the country, built up over a long period, and aiming at the destruction of key factories. Gott has been more talkative than any of the others. He says that Lewis had promised them action this week—this Friday, in fact—and that the trouble in this country will coincide with a wave of strong anti-British sentiment in the United States.'

Loftus kept quite still.

'Does he specify what damage and what factories?'

'No. He claims that only Lewis knew.'

'Does anything that Lewis told you bear out that probability?' asked Whitterly.

Loftus said slowly: 'Ye-es. He said that all preparations

were made, and that we had no idea of them. I thought he was boasting or bluffing, but it could be true.'

'Damn it!' exploded Scott, 'if that's happened under our eyes, with none of you people having the faintest suspicion, it's criminal negligence. We should know what's happening here, even if we can't get details of what's happening abroad. What *is* the matter with our Intelligence?'

Hershall broke in.

'Let's keep to the point. You obtained no details from Lewis, Loftus?'

'No.'

'Manfrey, Gott or Pellisser must know something,' interjected Scott. He was quick-tempered, but a man for whom Loftus had considerable respect.

Loftus shook his head.

'That isn't likely, sir. In fact it's obvious that Lewis wanted to get rid of the trio. If they were likely to know anything of particular value he would surely have shot them before he left.'

'It sounds absurd,' said Scott. 'How could he use them if they knew nothing?'

Craigie broke in.

'They're directors of a big distributing company, and Lewis told them their organisation would be invaluable when the time came to strike. They have received big sums from Argentina.'

'Argentina or Lewis?' asked Loftus.

'It amounts to the same thing,' said Whitterly.

'Ye-es. It could be,' said Loftus; but he sounded sceptical.

'Only could be?' Hershall flashed.

Loftus said: 'I don't think we should take anything for granted yet.'

'I don't know what you're talking about,' said Scott. 'These damned traitors have admitted what they were doing. We now know we've a powerful Neo-Nazi organisation in the country, with a sprinkling of quislings. Manfrey, Gott and Pellisser are all well-known business men. If they'd link up with this blasted ring, so would others. Who *are* the others?—they must know, and it's the crucial problem.'

'They say they know only Lewis,' said Craigie.

'Give me five minutes alone with them,' snapped Scott, 'and I'd beat the truth out of their hides.'

'As far as I can see,' said Hershall, raising a deprecating hand in Scott's direction, 'Loftus isn't yet convinced that there *is* any such widespread organisation—isn't that so, Loftus?'

'It is,' said Loftus firmly. 'I don't believe that one could be so widespread without some suspicion of it reaching Whitterly's men, or ours. But some sort of lesser organisation there must be—and Lewis is in it. He's served a clever trick on us by handing over Manfrey and Company, but we should be able to see round it. We've one or two fairly obvious pointers. Lewis has made it clear that the girl is dangerous, and stated that Hoppermann could delay him for a short time. So we may get a lead from Hoppermann or his daughter.'

'*May* get a lead,' snorted Scott. 'We *must* get one.'

Hershall took his cheroot out of his mouth.

'Loftus, I want you to interrogate Manfrey and Company, as you call them. Craigie, you and Whitterly will do everything possible to find whether there is danger of anything happening in the country on Friday. To-morrow, that is, since it's Thursday morning now,' he added crisply. 'You haven't much time.'

1 4

TALK WITH CHRISTINE

Bill Loftus was tired.

It was two o'clock on that Thursday afternoon, and he had not seen bed for forty-odd hours. He had been more than ordinarily busy, and he had felt an overwhelming need for sleep even before seeing Hershall, Scott and Whitterly, but it had not been possible.

He had spent several hours interrogating Gott, Pellisser and Manfrey. They knew, they said, that Lewis had many others with him, but they did not know their names. They could give details of nothing. Their task had been to maintain their own organisation, one specialising in the distribution of retail goods, and possessing one of the biggest fleets of lorries in the country, in perfect condition, ready for immediate action.

Lewis had not taken them into his confidence, but he had told them, three days before, that Hoppermann's arrival might cause trouble and delay. He had, in fact, made them thoroughly nervous.

He had also deliberately handed them over to the authorities, contriving it in a way which made it certain that they would be forced to confess what they knew.

Why?

There were other things Loftus had to discover, however, and after the questioning he had seen Hoppermann, who had gone to the American Embassy and now seemed prepared to stay there indefinitely. There was little doubt that his experience the previous night had jolted the American badly. He asked again for Loftus to accompany him personally on his tour, and persisted in his refusal to be served by the Errols.

Loftus left it at that.

Hoppermann declared that he had never heard of Lewis, that after being taken to Lester Drive he had been locked in a room seeing no one but the manservant, Blake. He was grateful for Loftus's last-minute intervention, and in saying so made Loftus feel almost embarrassed.

'I should have listened more to you from the start, I guess.'

'Let's forget that, shall we? About your London office, Hoppermann—how long has Sell been the manager?'

'For eight years.'

'Has he always given satisfaction?'

'Eight years, I said, not eight weeks! No man who doesn't give me satisfaction stays on my pay-roll for that length of time.'

'The same applies to Goss, I take it?'

Hoppermann hesitated, and Loftus waited, wondering whether he was going to be told the truth about that plain-speaking American who showed no reluctance at declaring that he believed the British were two-timing scoundrels. There was a long pause, and Loftus remembered that Hoppermann had started to describe Goss in one way, and actually done so in another.

'I guess I owe you this,' said Hoppermann. 'Goss is my personal bodyguard, Loftus.'

Loftus said: 'How long has he held that post?'

'Oh, for five or six years.'

'Does he really think the way he talks?'

'He's sincere, I guess.'

Loftus leaned forward.

'There is one more thing I'd like you to clear up. I've had reports that others who are with you in trying to change the President's policy are scared out of their lives.'

The American looked squarely at him.

'Here it is, as straight as I can give it. All men of authority are liable sooner or later to be threatened, and some of the men working on my Committee—you know about my Committee?'

'The one for Doing the Doublecross on England, yes.'

Hoppermann coloured.

'I wish you wouldn't be so bitter. They think they're being threatened by British agents.'

There was another, longer pause, while Loftus read into the American's words all that had been omitted. The Committee—Loftus did not remember its full title, but it implied making sure that America was not taken advantage of—*believed that its members were being threatened by the English, to make them withdraw their opposition to the N.A.T.O. Alliance.*

'Do you really think that?'

'It isn't impossible,' said Hoppermann.

'You seriously think that this country would attempt to adopt gangster-methods against prominent Americans because of their lack of sympathy with us?'

Hoppermann said nothing.

'All right,' said Loftus at last. 'We'll leave it at that. Now, just one other thing, please. Your daughter—'

Hoppermann said sharply: 'I've told you, we're not on good terms.'

'Have you any idea why she should be victimised?'

'None at all,' Hoppermann assured him. 'I haven't seen her in three years, Loftus. I've been thinking around it. It looks as if this man Lewis thought she might be able to give the low-down on me, but he was all wrong.'

'That wouldn't explain the second show,' said Loftus. 'He intended to kill her. I'll go further, and say he's frightened of her.'

'That's baloney,' said Hoppermann.

'We'll see. Now, this time—' a faint smile played at his lips —'can I rely on you to stay here, or not to venture out without Goss and my men? I've detailed two, the Errols I told you about, to wait here for you, and be ready any time you want them.'

'I don't like being followed,' said Hoppermann.

'Try to overcome the dislike,' said Loftus dryly.

Robert Carruthers, known more popularly among Department agents as Carry, boasted that he had never been in love.

There was something in that, moreover. Carruthers, while popular with women, was not a ladies' man, and for that reason Loftus had arranged for Carruthers to go to see Christine Weston as soon as the hospital gave permission. Permission being granted about four o'clock that Thursday afternoon Carruthers entered the small private ward of the nursing home, expecting to find the girl in bed, and looking very much the worse for her misadventures. Instead he found her sitting in an easy chair, in a dressing-gown, and with blankets gathered about her legs, tucked under her feet to make sure she was not in a draught.

Her eyes were tired-looking, the pupils mere pinpoints.

Christine Weston, *née* Hoppermann, had expected to see Loftus. There had been something about him she had not properly understood. Somehow he had seemed to know how she thought of the loss of her husband. That was an old tragedy now, old as far as speed of events in modern days was concerned; but its wound was still raw.

She had been looking forward to seeing Loftus, and the sight of the tall, fair-haired Carruthers, a good-looking man with a rather tentative smile, disappointed her. Carruthers saw that.

'Hallo,' he said. 'I'm not what you expected. Never mind.' He pulled a chair up and sat down. 'How about giving me a résumé of what happened after you left Loftus?'

She nodded, paused for a moment, then began her story. It was very much as Loftus had suspected.

She and her father had climbed into the cab only to find a man sitting in the back of it, covering them with a gun. They had driven to the Barnes house, Hoppermann had been forced out, and she had been unable to move because her ankles had been hobbled. Before leaving the cab the man with the gun had scratched her arm, apparently by accident. She had not thought a lot of it at the time, but after half-an-hour she had lost consciousness, and she remembered nothing more until waking up in the nursing home.

Carruthers looked grave. 'There isn't any doubt that they proposed to kill you.'

She shivered. 'But why on earth should they?'

'Is there anything you know about Lewis which might put him in a spot?'

'There can't be. I've never heard of him.'

'Well, his friends then. Do you know Lord Manfrey, Sir Geoffrey Gott or Gabriel Pellisser?'

'I think I met Gott someplace,' admitted Christine, 'but I don't really remember.'

'Do you know many people in England?'

'I've lived here for nearly three years.'

'Your own friends, or your husband's?'

'Mostly his.'

'I suppose there couldn't be a list of them?' said Carruthers. 'We have to find the link between you and Lewis, and it seems that it can only be through friends.'

Christine sat back a little in her chair, and carefully adjusted the folds of the blanket about her knees.

'All this is nonsense,' she said decisively. 'You're suggesting that I've learned something of vital importance by accident. It's—'

'Don't say fantastic!' appealed Carruthers. 'Nonsense and absurd cover it well enough!' He grinned. 'The fact remains that they wanted to put you out, so presumably you can be dangerous to them. We can't get round that. Did you know your father was coming to England?'

'Only from the Press.'

'Did you ever visit the London office?'

'To see the manager.'

'Sell?'

'Yes, that's right. I have a fairly large block of Nu-Steel Shares—they were left me by my grandfather. Sell wanted to buy. Father always disliked having anyone who was not at his beck-and-call owning the Corporation's stock.'

'Did you sell?'

'No; why should I? They're going up.'

'Yes, I'll say they are,' said Carruthers. 'A small fortune

could be won from a little manipulation in Nu-Steel shares over the past five or six years, couldn't it?'

'They've been getting progressively stronger, yes. But I don't see where this is leading us to.'

Carruthers smiled. 'No, and quite honestly, nor do I. My big *forte* is memory—it's nearly photographic, and I shall go back to Loftus and report. If there's anything to be made out of it, he'll do it.'

'You seem very confident in Loftus.'

'Great Scott, yes!' said Carruthers. 'The man is a positive genius. He's a bit off at the moment; socially, I mean.' It was strange, thought Christine Weston, that for a moment—it passed very quickly—he looked much as Loftus had looked, and there were shadows in his eyes. 'You haven't heard?'

'Heard what?'

'He was engaged. She was in the business, and followed your father, or so she thought, in the airliner. Loftus didn't know about it until yesterday.'

Christine lost some of her colour. 'I—I see.' Her voice was very low. 'I'm terribly sorry.'

'Can't be helped,' said Carruthers, awkwardly. 'Well, I'll get along. You'll probably find Loftus here soon.'

'I'll be glad to see him,' said Christine slowly.

At eight o'clock that evening, Loftus telephoned Christine Weston at the nursing home.

'Hallo, Mrs. Weston. Loftus here . . . These Nu-Steel shares you talked about. Where do you keep them?'

'At my flat.'

'Are they in a safe?'

'No, there isn't one. They're in a strong-box, under the bed. But why—'

'It's just an idea,' said Loftus. 'I'm going to burgle your flat. You don't mind, do you?'

'I don't—' she gasped the words, then said more collect-edly: 'I'd rather like to be there.'

'Oh, no.' said Loftus. 'There's no time for it, and it would spoil our form, anyhow. I'll report as soon as we've finished—with any luck at about nine o'clock.' He rang off and there was more than a hint of excitement in his manner as he turned to Ned Oundle. 'Ned—you and I are off to 120, Bay Court, Park Lane. And we're in a hurry. Carry, 'phone two or three of the lads and have them come over in support. You make it, too.'

In just under eight minutes Loftus had drawn up outside Bay Court and was showing a commissionaire his Special Branch card and demanding the master-key which would get him into Christine Weston's flat. There was only a short delay before the manager escorted Loftus and Oundle upstairs in person. Outside the flat the man paused.

'You quite understand, gentlemen, that this responsibility is wholly that of the police?'

'Yes, fully,' said Loftus. 'Do you mind if I—'

He did not go on, for the door opened before he took the key from the manager's hand.

Two men came out at high speed. One was a thug of the Stocker *genre*. The other Loftus recognised immediately as the little man who had tried to kill Hoppermann with the hand-grenade.

The little man had a gun; the thug was carrying a large metal box.

15

PREVENTION BETTER THAN CURE

The little man fired.

It happened that he jogged his elbow against the thug, and the bullet which should have gone through Loftus's chest went instead through the shoulder of the manager. The man uttered a gasp and staggered back against the wall, swung round by the force of the shot.

Loftus hit the little man.

The blow did not carry full weight, but it was enough to take the fellow off his balance, and send him staggering back against the thug. Oundle had taken the wise course, and retreated a few yards along the passage, gun in hand. Loftus reached over the little man's head, and contrived to get his fingers about the thug's throat.

His grip tightened, and he crowded in, while Oundle, seeing that there was no immediate danger of an escape, went forward. Between them, they had the men disarmed and in the flat within three minutes.

The manager was half-conscious, and muttered:

'There— there is a house doctor. Please—'

'Ring for him, Ned,' said Loftus.

Oundle went to a telephone in the room to do so. Loftus turned and eyed the little man and the thug, both of whom were in easy chairs. They sat as far back in them as they could, the bigger of the two men obviously scared out of his wits, the other, with his eyes closed, going through one of the performances which he had shown at Hoppermann's office. Loftus waited until Oundle had telephoned for the doctor and bent over the manager, and then approached the little man.

Before he spoke, there was a sharp knock at the door.

He opened it cautiously, and was relieved to see Carruthers, closely followed by Grey and Dunster, and a younger agent called Graham. Loftus explained the situation quickly, and the men made free of Christine's flat. It was a three-roomed one, with a good view over Hyde Park from the lounge window, and it passed through Loftus's mind that she must have an ample income.

One of the three rooms was obviously a bedroom set aside for visitors; there were no clothes in the wardrobe. Loftus used this room for his interrogation of the gunman, whom he had lifted bodily from the easy chair in which he lay back, feigning unconsciousness. Loftus put him face-downwards on the bed, and slapped his shoulder. The man jumped and turned over.

Loftus looked at him without speaking.

The prisoner now abandoned all attempts at pretence and sat bolt upright on the bed, one hand a little behind him.

'Who sent you here?'

'Find out,' said the little man.

'What did you come for?'

'Find out.'

'What is your name?' asked Loftus stonily.

'Find out,' said the little man in the same monotone.

'You have much to learn,' said Loftus. 'You can talk now, and freely, or you'll talk later when you can't form the words so easily, and when you're wishing you were dead.' He too spoke in an even voice, a cold one, and he knew that the method of speaking scared the man, whose eyes moved towards the window.

'I—I won't say a thing.' There was bravado in the words and in the manner. Loftus shrugged, and lit a cigarette. When it was glowing redly, he took it from his lips, stepped forward, and, although the other tried to wriggle away, pinioned him to the bed where he was unable to do more than squirm under the weight of Loftus's left arm and hand.

Loftus lowered the cigarette towards the man's cheek.

'This isn't a joke,' he said. 'Who are you?'

The man kept quite still, as if fascinated. Loftus wondered, in a curiously detached frame of mind, whether the fellow would hold out until the cigarette actually did touch him. He did not think it likely, and when the glow must have been warm against the sallow cheek, the man gasped.

'No, don't, don't do that!'

Loftus kept the cigarette still.

'What is your name?'

'Gug-Guggleheim,' said the little man, gasping each syllable out desperately. 'Guggleheim!'

'Who sent you?'

'Lewis.'

'What for?'

'The—the shares.'

'What shares?'

'The Nu-Steel Corporation.'

'I see. Why does Lewis want them?'

'I don't know, I swear I don't know!'

Loftus paused, and he saw fear in his prisoner's eyes, fear

because the little man thought he might not be believed. He said slowly:

'I'll accept that, for the moment. Why did you go to see Hoppermann at his office?'

'Lewis sent me. I was to—' began Guggleheim.

A sharp tap on the door interrupted him. Loftus cursed under his breath, but stepped forward and opened the door, keeping one eye on Guggleheim, who lay quite still, showing no inclination to bolt for it. Ned Oundle was standing in the other room, and by his side was the thin, perfumed figure of A. J. Sell, the Hoppermann London manager.

Sell's voice was shrill, either with fear or indignation.

'I want to know what this means! This flat belongs to Mrs. Weston, you have no right here.'

'Have you?' asked Loftus.

'I called to see her. Where—where is she?'

'Busy,' said Loftus. 'What do you want to see her about?'

'It is a matter of business,' said Sell.

Loftus smiled grimly. 'Your business with Mrs. Weston can wait. Why did you come?'

'I refuse completely to make any statement to *you*. I shall get in touch with her at once, and—'

'Make another offer for the shares,' said Loftus evenly. He scored a direct hit.

'How did you know of that?'

'A little bird told me,' said Loftus. 'I shall want to question you later, Mr. Sell, but you may go now.'

He nodded to Oundle, who gripped Sell's right arm above the elbow and hustled him away. Loftus closed the door and turned back to Guggleheim. Even though he knew Ned had been quite right to disturb him, he confounded the interruption. Guggleheim had now had time to prepare his story.

He sat on the end of the bed.

'We were talking about your visit to Hoppermann,' he said.

'Yes,' said Guggleheim glibly. 'I had to go and throw a scare into him, that's all, and pretend I was anti-Yank.' He sniffed. '*And* I am. I guess—'

'Guggleheim,' said Loftus, shaking his head. 'You aren't making things any easier for yourself by not telling me the truth. I think—'

He did not see any movement, or any shadow, he did not hear a sound until there was a crack at the window, and looking round abruptly he saw glass breaking. He ducked but kept his eyes towards the window. He saw a man standing outside, and knew then there must be a fire-escape there. He saw the gun in the man's hand, and he heard Guggleheim screaming:

'No, no, I wasn't going to talk, I wasn't—'

He saw two flashes of flame.

He heard Guggleheim scream again, and then go very silent.

He saw the figure by the window turn towards him, gun in hand, but in those few seconds of concentrated action, Loftus had reached his own gun, and he fired through his pocket.

A sharp cry followed, and the man staggered to the edge of the fire-escape. Loftus saw him lurch heavily against the safety rail and then topple from sight.

Loftus reached the window.

Loftus heard his scream, loud at first, and then gradually fading.

He did not look over the edge, and did not hear the thud, although from below he heard the screeching of brakes, an occasional shout, and the shrill blast of police whistles.

He turned back to the room.

Guggleheim was lying quite still, with two holes in his

forehead. They bled surprisingly little. Then the door opened abruptly to admit Oundle.

Loftus spoke in a low, hard voice.

'I had him in front of my eyes, and I lost him, Ned. I think I must be losing my grip.'

'Don't be a fool,' said Oundle tartly. He took the situation in quickly, and began to close the window. 'If there was a customer waiting there you didn't have a chance.'

'I should have looked outside the window,' said Loftus. 'Oh, well.' He pressed a hand to his forehead as if wearily. 'How's the manager?'

'He'll come through,' said Oundle. 'He's been moved to a hospital, Bill, don't worry about him. Young Graham's tagging Sell. Grey and Dunster are taking care of our friend with the steel box. And Carruthers is having a look round. Let's see what he's found.'

Loftus followed Oundle back to the sitting-room. The weariness, almost depression, which had so suddenly assailed him, had passed.

'Dunster, you and Grey had better take this customer to Brook Street. I'll be along as soon as I can.'

'Right' said Dunster. With Grey, he regarded Loftus with more than a degree of hero-worship, and he had learned to jump to Loftus's orders.

As soon as the door had closed, Loftus and Oundle joined Carruthers in a systematic search of the flat. It was quick but comprehensive, and no trained police-worker could have made a tidier job of it.

Little was found. What few letters there were, Loftus discovered in a locked writing-case, the key of which was in a dressing-table drawer; three in a firm, masculine handwriting, with two-year-old postmarks, which he rightly imagined were the last letters Christine had received from her husband; a letter from Sell, asking her to call on him, and dated a week before; and two letters from her mother, in New York. Apart from a copy of a marriage certificate, that was all.

Loftus put them back, and relocked the writing-case.

'Now we'll try the box,' he said.

That was a different proposition, for this time they were unable to find the key. Loftus spent five minutes prising at the lock with a skeleton-key, and had decided that he had either to take the box to Christine, or else have it forced, when there was a sharp ring at the front bell.

'Open up, Carry, will you?' Loftus was still bending over the box.

Carruthers opened the door, and a woman said:

'Good evening. I wonder if I may come into my flat.'

16

LOFTUS GETS A HUNCH

There was weariness in Christine Weston's voice, but, although Loftus watched her closely, he could detect no sign of apprehension.

'Forgive us, Mrs. Weston. I did tell you that I was coming and I hoped you realised I was worried about the safety of your shares. I had cause to be. We met two gentlemen who were coming away, one with your strong-box tucked under his arm.'

She sat down a little heavily on the arm of a chair.

Loftus felt he owed it to her to tell her just what had happened, and he did so without further waste of time. When he had finished, she looked at him, but did not speak.

'As you know,' said Loftus a little diffidently, 'there's plenty of room at my flat. Perhaps—' He tailed off.

She hesitated.

'Is that another way of saying you propose to keep an eye on me all the time?'

'We'd have you watched, anyhow.'

'All right,' she said. 'Thank you. I'll be glad to come. And I suppose you'd rather talk there?'

'I think so,' said Loftus. 'If you care to pack a few things, and bring the key to the strong-box, we'll get away.'

Once they were back in Loftus's flat, the box was opened. The contents were intact.

Loftus frowned.

'Guggleheim died just as he was about to tell me what happened at the office, that's reasonably certain. It was vital that I shouldn't know the whole truth of that episode, and so he was killed. If we can find exactly what your father is playing in this, we shall be at least half-way to the truth. We're already one step forward. Sell wanted to buy the shares, but did he want them for your father or for someone else?' He paused. 'Mrs. Weston, do you know much of the Hoppermann company's affairs?'

'Not a great deal.'

'How strong are they?'

'If you mean are they on the rocks, you've started looking the wrong way, Mr. Loftus. The company was good even in the depression days, and since the big British and American war orders, it's bigger and sounder than ever. I'd say my father was worth every penny of fifty million dollars.'

Loftus widened his eyes.

'Is he, by George! Wholly in Nu-Steel?'

'Practically all of it, yes.'

Loftus looked at her for some seconds, then jumped to his feet, 'I'm going to see Craigie. Excuse me, Mrs. Weston.'

Loftus stepped into Craigie's office, half-closing his eyes against the bright light. Craigie was sitting at his desk, and he looked up with a smile. 'Hallo, Bill. I've got a message for you from young Graham. He says he's tailed your friend Sell to 75, Fern Mansions, Victoria.'

'Good work,' said Loftus. 'I'm beginning to think we *might* be getting somewhere.' He explained what had happened, leaving nothing unsaid.

'It could be an endeavor to get control of American steel, and other industries. Supposing—just supposing—that someone thinks there's a good chance of getting control of Hoppermann Inc., and several of the other corporations? I've been thinking of the Committee of which Hoppermann is chairman. There's du Pacq of Atlantic Coast Shipping, Inc., Stevenson of U.S.A., Brown—but I needn't go into details, you know them as well as I do. Representatives of all the major industries—shipping, radio, steel, electronics—there's at least one representative from all those trades on this Committee. Then there are some other angles we could look at with advantage. Guggleheim knew why he was sent to Hoppermann's office, and he was killed to stop him talking.'

'I've seen the importance of that,' said Craigie slowly. 'Hoppermann is the key, or the only one we can see.'

'As Mrs. Weston and I decided. We must have great minds, we're thinking so much alike. Well, I've made you *au fait* with the ideas that are running about inside me, and now I'll get after Sell. One of the others tagged him. Young Graham.'

Loftus stopped, and frowned.

'Now what's the matter?' asked Craigie.

Loftus said slowly: 'I don't really know, Gordon. I had a peculiar hunch, and we might call it a vision. Trouble between England and America. I was just thinking that a good place to start trouble would be at the Embassy, and it might be an idea if the place were watched very closely. Hoppermann's taking refuge there, remember. *Supposing* there was a shindy outside the American Embassy? A demonstration against the States? I think the American Embassy should be very closely watched, old man.'

Craigie was already lifting the telephone.

Loftus went out and hurried down the stairs, along the narrow street, and into Whitehall. He knew that Dunster and Grey would have taken their prisoner to the second flat at Brook Street—Diana's old flat—and he telephoned it from a call-box. Dunster answered.

Loftus said: 'Ask Carruthers to look after the prisoner, Dunster, and come along with Grey, to Fern Mansions, Victoria. It's a big block, just off Victoria Street.'

'I remember,' said Dunster.

He worked with speed, for in twenty minutes Loftus saw his car pull up outside the entrance to that part of Fern Mansions where Flat 75 was situated. He paused for a moment, to allow Dunster and Grey to catch him up, and the three men walked into the building together.

They found Graham on a settee against the wall of a landing. Flat 75 was only a few yards along a carpeted passage. He straightened up when he saw Loftus, and Loftus asked quietly:

'Has he been here all the time?'

'Yes, he hasn't stirred since he came back.'

'Has anyone called on him?'

'No,' said Graham. 'Neither back nor front. After I phoned Craigie I phoned for some help. The flat's watched back and front, and I just had word that it's all quiet at the back.'

There was no reply to Loftus's first ring, nor his second, and he frowned. Dunster and Grey were waiting a little way along the passage, in case of emergency. Loftus rang again, and then turned.

'Slip down to the porter, one of you, and get a master-key,' he said.

Graham returned with a grey-haired porter who did not appear to have much regard for anyone, Special Branch policemen or not, who wanted to get into a flat with a master-key. He would have developed his theme to some length, but Loftus cut him short.

'Mr. Sell came in some time ago, and hasn't left since.'

'Well, supposin' 'e don't want visitors?'

'Supposing you want to save yourself from a charge of obstructing the police?' snapped Loftus.

The man sniffed.

'You ain't got no uniforms, 'ow do I know 'oo you are?'

Despite his argument, however, he produced a master-key, and Loftus opened the door.

He stepped into a small, empty hall-way.

Three doors led from it, and all three were closed. He looked about him for a moment, and then said to Graham:

'Watch the outer door, old man. You two stay put.' He spoke to Grey and Dunster as he opened one of the doors, looking into a lounge-cum-dining room which was furnished with a slightly flamboyant taste, not surprising in Mr. A. J. Sell. In fact, Loftus thought, the only thing surprising was the air of affluence, and the fact that Sell could apparently afford a large flat in a block where rents would run very high.

Could Hoppermann's London manager afford a luxury flat?

He shrugged, closed that door, and opened the next.

He stood quite still, staring at the body which was lying face-downwards on the floor, one leg twisted beneath the other. There was a very faint smell of almonds in the room, a smell Loftus recognised immediately; it was the characteristic odour of potassium cyanide.

Sell looked as if he had lain like that for a long time.

17
DEATH OF SELL

L oftus kept still, until Dunster called:
'What is it, Bill?'

'It's all right,' said Loftus slowly. 'Stay where you are for a moment.' He stepped forward and approached the window; it was open a few inches, and the smell of cyanide was no more pronounced near the body than it had been by the door. It was reasonable to believe that the potency had gone, that there was no danger to any of them. But he opened the window more widely before turning back to Sell.

He held his breath, and went down on one knee.

When he turned the man over he saw the distorted features, the terrible contortions of the lips and cheeks. Sell had died quickly, but in dreadful pain.

His right hand clutched a glass, which had not broken when hitting the carpet, in his fingers.

Loftus straightened up, and looked about the room. Sell was lying in front of the fireplace, and on the mantel-shelf was a tin of effervescent salts, with the lid open, and by it a spoon covered with a white powder. Loftus tightened his lips.

There was no doubt of what had happened.

Sell had come back from Bay Court, taken his saline, and had, at one gulp, swallowed enough cyanide to poison a dozen men.

He had been killed, moreover, by someone who knew his habit of taking the salts regularly; someone who had known that Loftus would probably be after him, and who had therefore made sure that he could not talk. The same someone had killed Guggleheim, *and who had wanted to make certain that Loftus did not learn who had tried to buy the Nu-Steel shares.*

Loftus went back into the hall.

The porter was standing by the outer door, glaring ill-temperedly at Loftus.

'Well, yer satisfied?' he demanded.

'Quite satisfied,' said Loftus shortly. 'Graham, go downstairs with this fellow, and telephone the Yard. If Superintendent Miller can't come himself, get someone who can.' He turned away as the porter opened his lips to make some further protest but changed his mind.

Dunster and Grey eyed Loftus keenly. He explained, briefly, and then said:

'We'll look through the flat while we've the chance, but I doubt if we'll find much. Someone was here in time to put the stuff in the tin, and I don't doubt he cleared out all the papers which might be interesting. Get a pillow-case, or something of the kind, Grey, and wrap that spoon, glass and tin, will you. Don't touch more than you need, there may be prints. Be careful with the powder, and don't let water touch it.'

Loftus and Dunster started to search the flat, and Loftus discovered a safe, hidden behind a water-colour picture. The door was not locked, but the safe was empty of everything save twenty-two pounds in one-pound notes, and some bank pass-books. Loftus glanced through the latter, not surprised to

find that they showed several recent payments to the credit of
A. J. Sell, each of five hundred pounds. Sell's salary payments,
of fifty pounds a month, were also recorded. The five hundred
pound items doubtless represented graft; but from whom?

It was not going to be easy to find out.

After the arrival of the police, to take charge of the flat and
to go through the routine which was not only necessary but
might, through finger prints or other clues, give results that
would help the Department, he went with a sergeant from
Scotland Yard to the house of the manager of Sell's bank, and,
after some trouble, arranged to be taken to the bank for a full
examination of the history of the account.

At one-fifteen a.m., Loftus learned that the five hundred
pound payments, paid quarterly over a period of one year, had
been in cash, and one pound notes at that.

Loftus pursed his lips.

'There isn't much chance of tracing them, I suppose?'

'Virtually none, sir,' said the manager, a prosy man and one
who behaved very well, in view of his having been dragged
from his bed in the early hours.

Loftus smiled.

'Thanks very much. I thought that was about the position.'

'May I know *why* these inquiries into Mr. Sell's account are
necessary?' demanded the manager. He paused, expectantly.

Loftus said: 'Mr. Sell was murdered to-night, sir, and we
want to find out by whom. Many thanks for your help. Good-
night.'

He turned up the collar of his coat, then went out into the
darkness of the Strand. The offices of Hoppermann, Inc., were
not fifty yards away. He wondered whether it would be wise
to visit them immediately, then remembered that the others
would probably be getting tired.

He went into a kiosk and made arrangements with Craigie

for the Errols to be relieved, for two other agents to replace Dunster and Grey, and for two more to be at Loftus's flat so that Carruthers and Oundle could get a few hours sleep. Then he asked Craigie to send Wally Davidson and Martin Best, two of the Department's oldest agents, to join him at the Hoppermann offices.

He waited in the doorway of the main building until they arrived, then opened the door with his skeleton-key, and all three men ran up the stairs to the second floor. Hoppermann's general office door gave Loftus no more trouble than the other had done.

They looked about the office where, by day, the typists and Jimmy Mayo sat at their desks. Loftus turned to Best. 'See that the door's locked, Martin, and put a booby-trap of some kind by it, in case others *get* interested. Anything will do so long as it'll make a noise if the door opens.'

He walked through the room and into Sell's office, producing a bunch of keys from his pocket.

Davidson followed him. 'What's that you've got?'

'The key to the safe, I hope,' said Loftus.

'How come?'

'I found them at Sell's flat,' said Loftus, twisting one of the keys off the ring. 'Try that bunch on the desk, will you?'

He tossed the remaining keys to Davidson, who busied himself finding the key which fitted the desk. Best came back with a grin on his face and smoke curling from a cigarette between his wide lips. He appeared to be amused by the earnestness with which Davidson worked, but his smile grew more tense as Loftus pulled open the door of the safe.

There were several files, some loose cash, and some bundles of share certificates. Loftus looked at the last first, and widened his eyes when he saw that they were not all of the Nu-Steel Corporation. There were some of the Atlantic Coast

Shipping Company, of U.S.A. Steel, and the Mid-West Electrical Corporation, and of the Texan Oil Company. The totals were comparatively small—each, in fact, represented one thousand ordinary shares, a small drop in the oceans of shares in the various companies.

Loftus folded the shares and tucked them into his pocket, where they made a large bulge in his coat. He ran through the other papers in the safe but found nothing of interest; mostly they were recent instructions from the States. The office, it seemed, was one solely of convenience, but Loftus was puzzled.

Why, for such a small flow of business, employ a comparatively large staff?

'I think we've got all we're going to from here. We'll get along.'

'I had hoped for fun and games,' said Best.

'It isn't going to surprise me if you get them,' said Loftus. 'And a little more than we really want, old son.' He re-locked the safe, then went through the outer room.

Best was dismantling a booby-trap made of chairs which must have collapsed if the door had been opened furtively, and so warned the others in ample time. He dropped a chair on his foot, and swore mildly. Loftus smiled absently, then, as the door opened, there came an unexpected sound; the telephone in the inner room rang.

The three men drew up.

Loftus said slowly:

'A wrong number, I wonder?'

'We'd better see,' said Davidson. 'Craigie might be wanting you.'

'Ye-es.' Best closed the door as Loftus went back into the private office. The telephone was still ringing, very loud in the silence. Loftus lifted the receiver and said in a quiet voice:

'Who is that, please?'

Had they not been watching him, the others would not have recognised Loftus from his voice.

And then they saw him start, saw his fingers tighten about the telephone.

Standing very still, Loftus heard a suave, familiar voice—the voice which he had first heard from Lewis. That itself was startling enough, but the words made him clench his teeth.

'If that is not Loftus,' said Lewis. *'I want to speak to him.'*

There was a moment of utter silence in the office. Best and Davidson crowded the door, wishing they could hear what was being said. Loftus's mind worked very quickly, and he decided that there was no object in maintaining any pretence. As he spoke he motioned to the others, to try to get the call traced from a line in the other room.

'Well, Lewis? If you've got anything useful to say, say it.'

He heard the man laughing, and he did not like the sound.

'I could say so much, but why should I?'

'Then why ring?' drawled Loftus.

'To make you realise that I knew where to find you,' said Lewis. 'You have been carefully watched all day, Loftus, and your exceptional good fortune won't be of any further use to you. I'm *most* glad you elected to visit Hoppermann's office.'

Loftus said: 'No one followed me.'

There was a short silence, and he believed it was because Lewis was startled by that statement. It was a reasonably accurate one; Loftus did not believe that he had been followed. His mind, working then at high pressure, was going through the only possibilities. The office buildings might have been watched, and thus his arrival seen, *or else someone in the building might know that he had arrived there.*

Lewis recovered himself quickly.

'You're quite wrong, Loftus, you have been followed all the

time.' His insistence on the point, an unnecessary insistence unless it was a lie he wished to make convincing, told Loftus that one of his two possibilities was fairly near the mark.

'All right,' he said. 'I've been followed. What then?'

'Wisdom, but too late,' said Lewis. 'You see, Loftus, preparations were made at the office to settle Hoppermann's account, and those arrangements can now serve for you. You won't get away, neither will your friends.'

He paused. Loftus covered the mouthpiece with his hand, and said aloud: 'Try the outer door, Wally.' He uncovered it, then heard Lewis say:

'You aren't talkative? I can hardly believe it, Loftus, talking seemed to be quite a point with you. Today is Friday.'

'And the day after tomorrow is Sunday.'

'You won't live to see it,' said Lewis, and there was a disturbing note of certainty in his voice. 'You won't even live to see tomorrow. I expect Manfrey and the others have told you that I promised them results for today. They won't enjoy them, but the results will come.'

Loftus said in a cold voice:

'When is the demonstration at the Embassy due?' He spoke as if he were quite sure that there would be a demonstration.

There was a short, tense silence, and he felt neither fear nor anxiety, but relief. So it *was* true. He waited a brief moment and then rang off.

He had heard the other telephone ring, and Wally speaking; he had also heard a banging at the door leading to the passage. He was not surprised when Martin Best came to the door, hard-faced.

'It's locked and blocked outside, Bill.'

'That's not unexpected,' Loftus said. 'Lewis is somewhere in the building, I fancy, or some of his people are. Can we get it down together, do you think?'

126

'I doubt it.'

'H'm Loftus was dialling Craigie's number. 'See what the windows are like, will you?' He finished as Best went to obey, and heard Craigie's dry voice.

'The Embassy idea was a good one,' Loftus said quickly. 'And today, I think, will see the start of it. I'm still at Hopper-mann's office, and—'

He stopped speaking, abruptly.

He stared hard for a moment at the empty desk in front of him, knowing that the line had suddenly gone dead: there had been a *click* at the other end, or somewhere along the line, and he was not surprised when, after two attempts, he failed to get further word from Craigie.

A cut line, probably; and as likely as not inside this office block.

Best turned back from the windows.

'Sheer to the ground,' he said. 'Let's try the others.'

He and Loftus hurried into the outer office, but here too there was no possibility of escape.

Suddenly the light went out in both rooms. The utter dark-ness froze all men into total immobility—then Loftus put a hand to his pocket, saying:

'Who else has a torch?'

'Me,' said Best.

'I've a small one,' said Wally faintly.

'Good,' said Loftus. 'Martin, stand by the window and do that dot-dash business—we want help, and a fire-escape up to the window is probably the only way of getting it.' He watched Best flicking his torch on and off towards the Strand; then, glancing at the door leading to the passage, he stiffened.

A bright light, red and lurid and straining the eyes, showed suddenly beneath the door, then disappeared. A moment later another flame, stretching ten feet into the room and singeing the carpet in front of their eyes, came in, to disappear like the first.

Before anyone could speak, a positive sheet of flame was coming under the door, running about the carpet as if in liquid form.

Loftus said in an odd voice.

'Liquid fire, that's nice. I wonder how long we've got?'

18
LEWIS LAUGHS

There was a momentary quiet in the room after Loftus had spoken, broken only by the hissing of the flames which were coming beneath the door with greater intensity, and darting about the room in small pools of fire. Both Loftus and Davidson knew that by then the passage outside must be an inferno, and there was no possible chance of getting away except by the windows.

Loftus looked quickly round the room.

'There's no water here, except a drop in a glass. Let's have the carpet up, old son.' He began to move the typists' desks on to a stretch of bare board, and then with Davidson he pulled at the carpet, stamping out two or three patches where it had caught fire. When they had it in a roll, Davidson asked:

'What's next?'

'We'll get it as close to the door as we can, after putting the desks into the other room. The more we block the doorway the longer the fire will take to get through.' Loftus spoke simply and without undue excitement. 'Martin, carry on flashing from Sell's window, will you, while we barricade the door. Our one chance is from outside. I hope there's someone about who can read Morse.'

They worked swiftly, until the outer office was denuded of furniture. Then, drawing the rolled up carpet as close to the door as they could while leaving a gap wide enough for them to get through, they went into the other room. The floor-boards of the outer office were blazing, and the fire was running about the floor in little rivulets which threatened at any time to seep through into the inner office. But when it met the carpet its progress was delayed. Closing the door, Loftus and Davidson piled the furniture up, so that the flames would have even more work to do before they could begin the destruction of this room also.

'Any luck, Martin?'

'I thought I saw someone flash "O.K.",' said Best gruffly, 'but I haven't seen anything since.' He shrugged.

It was growing unbearably hot. Loftus took his coat off, taking out the share certificates and stuffing them into his waist-band.

'We mustn't lose the evidence,' said Wally, but despite the elaborate casualness of his voice Loftus could see he was feeling the strain.

Suddenly Loftus saw a flash of flame on a level with them, at a window opposite. Then came a *ping*! as a bullet struck the wall inside the room, opposite their own window.

All three men stepped hastily to the sides of the window as a stream of bullets came through from the building opposite. They could hear the thudding of lead against the piled furniture, and they could hear the roar of the fire in the adjoining room.

Loftus turned to the others. 'Why don't we have a shot at them?'

He took an automatic from his pocket and, when the

shooting stopped, went into sight and fired four times. He did not know whether he had any luck—and he did not know that, as the gunman by the other window hastily backed out of the way, Lewis laughed.

It was the 'second' Lewis, the big and bulky Lewis. He was standing in a room opposite that of the Hoppermann Company, and he laughed loudly, until one of the gunmen with him muttered under his breath. Lewis did not hear what he said; he would have ignored it even if he had.

Between gales of laughter he called softly:

'Getting desperate, Loftus? Enjoying it, Loftus?'

But of this Loftus knew nothing. All he could hear was the roaring of the flames, which was getting louder and louder.

The sound of a fire-engine bell would have given him and the others more pleasure than anything in the world, but there was no hint of it. It seemed that Best's signals had not been understood, and that until the fire was seen there would be no possibility of escape—by which time it might be too late.

The three men were bathed in sweat, their throats parched, their mouths dry. The furniture they had so carefully piled against the door was now blazing, the flames no more than twenty feet away and already beginning to lick their way along the floor and the wainscoting. In a curiously detached frame of mind, Loftus estimated that they had no more than ten minutes grace.

And then they heard the bell.

It came clanging along the Strand, and they heard its engine roaring more and more loudly. Then it stopped, and Loftus went cautiously to the window. He withdrew his head quickly, for gunfire immediately started from the opposite building. He tightened his lips, knowing that however quickly the firemen worked the position remained hopeless while the gunmen still operated, and he saw no way of giving warning.

Was it possible that the shooting had been seen from the road?

It was not a thing to rely on, Loftus knew.

All at once his mind refused to work, refused to go beyond the logical acceptance of the likely conclusion to this fight with Lewis. It was peculiar to feel a certainty that he was at the end of his run, to react fatalistically to it, virtually resigned to losing. But he had managed to let Craigie know that the guess at trouble at the Embassy was right, and he believed that Craigie would be able to go on from there, that Lewis's triumph would only be a temporary one.

It was insufferably hot.

Breathing was difficult, and he felt sweat running down his back. He saw the grotesquely smoke-blackened flame-illuminated figures of Martin Best and Wally Davidson, men who had been in the Department before he had joined. He wished he could say something to them.

Then Wally shouted: 'Look!'

There was no need for the cry; the others saw as quickly as he the brilliant beam of light which shot from a building alongside that in which they were trapped, and shone for a moment on three men in the window opposite. Two whom Loftus did not recognise, and *Lewis*!

Lewis's lips were parted, and he drew back out of the glare, his hand raised to cover his face. Then he turned, while from the building alongside Loftus there came the rat-tat-tat of a tommy-gun. The three figures disappeared, but whether they were hit or whether they had dodged back was uncertain. The tommy-gun continued to rattle, as the searchlight played its bright beam on the window at which they had been seen.

The fire-engine had stopped immediately below, and at once the escape-ladder was swaying outside the window of Hoppermann's office. The three Department Z men stared down at it. But the flames were licking the floor just behind them, and their clothes were singeing. Their escape would be touch and go, even now.

It was a period of such concentrated tension that they lost all count of time.

Only vaguely did Loftus hear the stutter of a car engine far below, and the shouts of firemen and police trying to stop the driver from coming past. Loftus did not see the man, or the car. But the latter came on swerving alongside the fire-escape, scattering the little crowd gathered by the engine.

The helmet of a fireman showed beneath the window.

Leaning out, Loftus gripped his wrist to help him inside. The fire grew nearer, but he believed that the crisis was over, that in a few minutes they would be quite safe.

Then he heard the explosion.

He did not see the man in the car throwing a small object towards the fire-escape, nor hear the shouts of the men nearby. He did see the flash of the explosion; but suddenly the fire-escape swayed away, gathering speed as it swerved down-wards, to crash in the street below. *The bottom section had been blown to pieces.*

The dead weight of the fireman fell suddenly on Loftus's arm. It came so abruptly that it almost carried Loftus out of the window; it would have done had Martin Best not made a grab at his waist.

They heard the ladder crash, while Loftus held the man dangling full-length out of the window. They saw the car then and the shooting which followed it, the firing from the tommy-gun ranged on their side. Loftus had no time to think, time only to realise that what had seemed the certainty of escape had been snatched away from them.

He hauled the man up, laboriously.

'Well, we can jump,' said Wally Davidson in a muffled voice.

'Jump, yes,' said Loftus. He saw that the men below were spreading out the net to catch them, realising that there was no time to run up another escape-ladder. He wondered in a queer way why he had not thought of that obvious jump-and-hope solution before. He pulled the man in, wondering whether they would make it. Five tall storeys to go down, and they were all heavy men.

The fireman clambered into the room. By now the flames were licking as far as the window, and the back of Loftus's coat had caught fire; Best beat it out.

The fireman, masked and breathing hard, gasped:

'Can—get up. Roof.'

Loftus said: 'Damnation, is that true?'

The question was rhetorical, nothing else, for promptly he put his foot on the window-sill and slowly steadied himself. He saw the ledge of the roof overhanging the window, and when he stretched up an arm he could grip the ledge with his hand. He put up his other hand, gripped again, and then pulled himself up.

Progress was agonisingly slow.

But it could be done, he realised, and he gritted his teeth, seeing everything above him very clearly in the lurid glare of the fire. He drew himself high enough to put a knee on the ledge, and then hauled himself onto the roof.

He saw another pair of hands gripping the ledge, and, going down on his stomach, leaned over and caught hold of the wrists, hauling Wally Davidson over. Best came next, the ends of his trousers smouldering. Loftus slapped at them, putting them out, while the fireman clambered after them.

Faintly they heard the cheering from below; and suddenly Loftus felt so light-hearted that he waved a hand to the crowd.

Then all four men crawled along the edge of the roof, and after forcing a sky-light window, found themselves in a corridor on the top floor of the adjacent building.

By the time they reached the hall on the ground floor, Loftus could hear the hiss of water being directed on the burning offices, and through an open door saw a dozen or more men.

One separated from the others and came hurrying into the hallway.

'Hallo, hallo,' he said, grinning widely. 'All safe and sound?'

Loftus stared. *Dunster!* He almost shouted the word, for he was surprised beyond measure. Wally and Best stared equally, and Dunster's grin grew a little embarrassed.

'I know I should be asleep,' he said, 'but I felt like hanging around when I knew where you were, and so I did. Er—as a matter of fact, I—'

'Out with it,' said Loftus encouragingly.

'As a matter of fact,' said Dunster with an effort, 'I saw the shooting on the other side and fixed it with a military unit to rig up the searchlight and the tommy-gun. It looked pretty grim, otherwise, and—'

He was interrupted by a warning shout from someone in the crowd.

There was a loud crack, a roar, and then an avalanche of tumbling debris from the top of the burning building. The men split up, suddenly aware again of danger. Best, Davidson and the fireman reached the roadway safely. Dunster followed them, Loftus a yard behind. A piece of masonry, not particularly heavy, but weighty enough, struck him a glancing blow on the head, and sent him pitching forward into unconsciousness.

* * *

It was daylight when he came round.

He was lying in a strange bed, in a small, green and white walled room, which smelt faintly of disinfectants. He frowned, grew aware that he had a headache and, putting a hand to his forehead, found that his head was bandaged.

Memory flowed back.

A few minutes afterwards a nurse came in, and he was told that he was in a nursing-home in South Audley Street. Hot on the nurse's heels came Doc Little.

'Hallo, Bill,' he said. 'When are you going to grow up?'

Loftus smiled.

'I've been asking myself that, old son. However, I'm still in the land of the living, and between you and me I feel pretty good, a mild headache excepted, and I think some tea and toast would send that away. I'm all right, aren't I? No bones broken and whatnot? I must be up and doing in an hour or two.'

Little smoothed the back of his head.

'If I had my way you'd stay where you are for a couple of days, but I know you won't. Craigie sent word that everything's being done that can be, and the others are all right.'

'What time is it?'

'About nine o'clock,' said Little airily.

'And how much more?' demanded Loftus suspiciously. He squinted down at Little's wrist-watch. 'It's half past ten, you congenital liar. I must be up at twelve; no later.'

'All right, all right,' said Little. 'I didn't expect you'd grown sensible over-night. I'll have some food sent in,' he added. 'And Dunster is waiting to see you—Craigie sent him over with a report.'

'Good man. I'll see him now.'

'And when you've finished and get on those two fool feet of yours, look in next door but one,' said Little. 'On the right.

Young Jimmy Mayo is there, and I've an idea he'll be glad to see you.'

'I won't forget,' promised Loftus.

He leaned back on his pillows, and greeted Dunster with a grin.

Dunster pulled up a chair.

'What have you got for me?' asked Loftus.

Dunster leaned back and closed his eyes, then began a comprehensive and detailed statement, including the fact that Lewis himself had escaped, but that the two gunmen had been hit; it would happen that way, thought Loftus a little bitterly. The story of the car which had driven at speed along the Strand, and from which a Mills bomb or its equivalent had been thrown at the fire-escape, was also told; the car had crashed, and its two occupants had been killed.

'That's good,' Loftus said slowly; but the news that Lewis had evaded capture filled him with disquiet.

'Good indeed,' said Dunster. 'Well, Miss—sorry, Mrs.— Weston is still at your flat. Craigie interviewed her, but she hasn't much more to say. Craigie says that he's following the angle suggested by the shares—we found some tucked in your trousers, and that apparently gave him an idea.'

Loftus frowned. 'We *must* get Lewis.'

Dunster grinned.

'That the shaggy customer who was in the window when we put the searchlight on last night?'

'Yes—did you see him?'

'I not only saw him, Bill, but I took a photograph. I usually carry a small Leica, y'know. How's that for a likeness?'

He took a print from his brief-case, and Loftus stared with increasing excitement at an excellent likeness of the 'second' Lewis.

'Craigie's getting the police to circulate it up and down the country,' Dunster said casually.

'Nice work. That makes it very much better all round,' said Loftus. 'I'd like to think we were going to get him inside twenty-four hours, but I suppose I mustn't ask for too much? I—Come in,' he called.

A tap on the door was followed by its slow opening, and then a nurse appeared, pushing a wheelchair. In the chair, his head raised and excitement in his eyes, his ginger hair fluffy and sticking well out from his head, was Jimmy Mayo.

'Hallo, hallo!' said Loftus heartily. 'Someone told you I was here, did they?'

'The doctor,' said Jimmy with a vast grin. 'Fancy us being in the same hospital, Mr. Loftus! Are you getting better?'

'Nearly as fast as you, I hope,' said Loftus. 'And you seem to be making first-class progress, old son. Have you had any more ideas?'

Jimmy grinned engagingly.

'Hang it, I'm on the sick-list!' His grin faded, and he looked a trifle wistful. 'I wish I could do something to help,' he said. 'It's a spy-ring, isn't it?'

'It looks very much like it,' said Loftus with the necessary gravity.

'I know a man who doesnt believe in spies,' said Jimmy. 'I've always told him different.'

'So I should think. Who is he?'

'Oh, Mr. Makin. You wouldn't know him. He's often in the office with Mr. Sell.'

Loftus stiffened. 'Is he, by Jove! How often?'

'Most days,' said Jimmy perfunctorily. 'He works just along the passage, you see—he's editor or something of the *Leather-craft Journal.* He's not a bad sort, I suppose, although I've heard him and Mr. Sell quarrelling sometimes. If I was Sell, I wouldn't stand for it.'

'No-o,' said Loftus slowly. He was in the grip of a fast increasing excitement as he went on: 'I'd like to hear more of Mr. Makin, old son. What does he look like?'

Jimmy, who had glanced down on the photograph of the 'second' Lewis, was no longer smiling but staring akin to excitement. He drew a deep breath, pointed to the photograph, and cried:

'Why, you know him. *That's* Mr. Makin!'

19

'THAT'S MR. MAKIN'

L oftus was thinking:

'Five minutes' talk with Jimmy or any of the girls in Sell's office would have told me about this, and I missed it. I *missed* it!' He leaned back on his pillows, and Jimmy said in a thinner voice, perhaps a little defiantly:

'It is, I know it is. You couldn't mistake him.'

Loftus pulled himself together.

'I don't doubt you for a moment, Jimmy, and you've helped us a lot more than you realise. You'll qualify for the Special Branch before you're much older! Wait half-a-mo', will you, while we get things done?' He turned to Dunster.

'Hurry along to Craigie's office, old man, and have several fellows go to the *Leathercraft* office, on the same floor as Hoppermann's. If there's any of it left, that is. Get all records, and go through them, particularly for names and addresses of subscribers. If the office is destroyed, try to get a list of subscribers, and any information that's possible about the place. All clear?'

'I'm nearly there,' said Dunster, pushing his chair back.

'Nice work, Jimmy! They told me you were hot, but I didn't think you'd be as hot as this.'

Jimmy's eyes were staring almost out of his head.

'Is—is this important?'

'This is nearly the most important thing there could be,' said Loftus, as Dunster went out. 'I think—' he stopped, for Dunster collided with something, and apologised; a feminine voice answered him, and immediately afterwards a nurse came in, pushing a small trolley. There was coffee, toast, bread-and-butter, and boiled eggs. He asked for another cup for Jimmy, and began to tell the boy as much as he could safely divulge—at the same time getting the story of 'Makin' and his frequent visits to Sell, not excluding the quarrels.

It seemed that Makin and Sell did some private business together; Jimmy had an idea it was to do with racing and betting, and he knew that Makin took some Football Pool coupons into Sells' office every week. The quarrels had been audible, but no one in the office knew anything about them beyond the fact that they frequently occurred.

Sell, it seemed, shouted the louder.

That was easily understandable, thought Loftus. Lewis would make demands which Sell disliked, and tried to avoid; Lewis would be quiet and dangerous, Sell would bluster with the raised, over-excited tones of a man who knows he has already lost the battle. Sell had been working with Lewis, mused Loftus, of that there was not the remotest doubt.

Sell had been eager to buy Christine's shares. And in his office Sell had shares of several of the other important American combines. In themselves these shares had been no more than a pointer, but Loftus now believed he saw beyond the pointer. Lewis and his principals—for there must be principals, were aiming to get as much control of the big American industrial corporations as possible. Leading members of some of those corporations were in fear of their lives, and Lewis and his principals had cleverly twisted the situation to make it look as if British agents were working on them to enforce their support for British aims.

It was taking shape.

And under the innocuous guise of Editor and Manager of the *Leathercraft Journal,* Lewis had kept in close and constant touch with Sell, who could doubtless influence a great number of the Nu-Steel shares.

Loftus prayed that the *Leathercraft* office had not been totally destroyed by the fire.

At half-past eleven the nurse came in to take Jimmy Mayo away; she brought with her a suit and other clothes for Loftus, all sent from his flat by Mrs. Weston, she told him.

An hour or so later, Loftus pulled up beside the damaged building, showed his private card to a sergeant on duty who had been told to allow a Mr. Loftus through, and then went in.

There was little to see from the outside, except the one gap from which the masonry had tumbled the previous night, and the harm done to the lower floors was negligible; but as he neared the fifth and top floor, Loftus could smell charred wood and rubber. When he arrived at the *Leathercraft Journal* office, he found that the outer door had been broken down.

But the floor was sound.

The passage further along was nothing but a mass of charred ruins, but the firemen had done a wonderful job, keeping the fire almost wholly to one side of the passage. Loftus went into the *Leathercraft* office; the office where, on the first day of the affair, Mark Errol had waited to watch Hoppermann; there was an ironic twist to that fact.

Dunster, Grey, Wally Davidson, Best and the Errols were there before him.

Files were open, the contents strewn about the office. The

men worked earnestly, and were putting certain papers—small cards, Loftus noticed—on one side.

They did not see him enter, and did not know he was there until he spoke.

'We've had a break, then?'

Dunster, nearest to him, looked up with a start.

'Why, hallo! Yes, we've had a break all right. Everything seems to be here, and it wouldn't have been discovered at all had the firemen not broken in.'

'Nice work,' said Loftus. 'And what have we found?'

'Well,' said Martin, 'the safe was crammed with shares of Nu-Steel, Atlantic Coast Shipping, Mid-West Electric—all the companies you'd thought about. Some of the shares were in Sell's safe, remember, and there are masses of them here.'

Loftus half sat on the corner of a desk.

'So we go on,' he said. 'And the subscribers?'

'They're filed in sections,' said Dunster quickly. 'One section is marked "A" and I fancy they're the gentlemen we want. There are more particulars about them, and—'

'They include a Mr. Guggleheim,' said Mike Errol.

'Not to mention A. J. Sell,' said Mark.

Loftus took a cigarette from his case slowly.

'Guggleheim and Sell, eh? I think we can safely tell the police to watch that list of subscribers.'

He felt a tremendous sense of contentment. It was working out the way he had expected. There was much that had to be settled, but he believed it would not take long. The germ of the plot was already in his hands, he had now to check and counter its ramifications. He saw the eager and satisfied faces of the others as they went on with the job of sorting and selecting, and he was filled with a warm feeling of kinship. Young Dunster and Grey, and the older men, had the same feeling; he knew that.

143

'Why not do something?' demanded Wally Davidson. 'We don't mind starting, but I don't see why you should sit and watch.'

'Hush?' said Best. 'He's thinking.'

'Dolts,' said Loftus. 'If you can't get through a simple job like that, I'll—'

He stopped abruptly, for he heard footsteps outside, and the protesting voice of a policeman. He thought for a moment that it meant interference; he would not have been surprised at another attempt to put the Department out of action. Instead, he saw Ned Oundle, and a policeman hurrying behind him. Ned's eyes were wide with more than ordinary excitement, and he snapped:

'Leave this and make it snappy, Bill. The Embassy trouble's started.'

20

HOSTILE DEMONSTRATIONS

I t transpired that Oundle had been one of the Department
men on duty outside the American Embassy, and that fact
told Loftus that the trouble could not have been prevented no
matter who had been there.

On the way in three cabs, with Oundle, Loftus and the
Errols in the first, Oundle said what he could about it. The
Leathercraft office had been cordoned off, and a strong guard
of police left there, although the 'A' subscriber cards were
tucked in the pockets of Loftus and the others.

'There was the usual crowd of passers-by, Bill, nothing
more. Then, before I knew where I was, a couple of dozen
men started throwing stones, and rushed the doors. The
dozens grew into hundreds pretty quickly.'

Loftus snapped: 'Did they get through?'

'Some of them, yes.'

'How many men did we have?'

'Twenty of our fellows, and twenty policemen. There's a
call out for the military, too.'

'So it's as bad as that,' said Loftus grimly.

'It was hotting up pretty fast when I left,' said Oundle.

Loftus nodded, and they were silent for the rest of the short journey.

The square was crowded.

Loftus's cabby went on as far as he could, blowing his horn freely, but it was clear that he could not approach the Embassy. Around the building, above which the Stars and Stripes was flying in a light breeze, was a dense mass of people, and from their throats was coming a deep roar.

Loftus heard loud voices roaring through megaphones.

'Where's Hoppermann? Where's Hoppermann?'

'Yanks go home!'

He wondered how many of these demented people were genuine fanatics, believing that America had failed in its duty. Fanatics and fools they might be, but they would never have been dangerous but for the way Lewis and his organisation had preyed on their minds.

Amongst the crowd was a more than liberal sprinkling of paid agents. He could tell some of them, wild-looking men, yelling and shouting and cursing. He heard screaming, too, from the few women in the crowd, women who were being trampled under foot. He saw policemen struggling to reach the Embassy, but from time to time a helmet disappeared, a man in blue was pushed under the horde of trampling feet. He saw a few soldiers with fixed bayonets, but they were not using the steel; they had not had orders, but unless this soon stopped, orders would surely have to be given. The crowd would be fired on, and a charge with fixed bayonets would become essential.

For the moment the mob had it.

Loftus and the others forced their way through towards the Embassy. They could see police holding the building itself, with some men in khaki, keeping back the surging crowd with truncheons and batons. Now and again a few people pushed their way through, but for the most part the thin line of police and soldiers kept the mob at bay.

Strained, white faces, glaring eyes, vicious oaths from innocent-looking men, unceasing parrot-cries, with one rising above all the others:

'Where's Hoppermann—*kill Hoppermann!'*

Loftus was at the head of his party. They had formed in a little group, and let nothing stand in their way. Men cursed as they were pushed aside, and a few stones and pieces of wood fell among them, but Loftus ignored the missiles.

He had a hand in his pocket about his gun—Oundle had given him one, Christine had not managed that—and he knew the others were doing the same. They could have drawn their weapons, but to start shooting then would be the height of folly, although it might become necessary to use them as clubs. He fingered the barrel of the automatic as, grimly and ruthlessly, he forced his way through.

'Kill Hoppermann, kill Hoppermann!'

'Yanks go home!'

A strong body of men grouped together, drawn back for a rush. A tall man whom Loftus thought he recognised had a megaphone.

'Now, then, altogether, we can get through. Find that bastard, that's all, find Hoppermann!'

No more than a dozen men were holding the gates, policemen, soldiers, three of the Deparment men. Most of them looked as if they had been hurt, three were bleeding from face wounds. The soldiers had lost their rifles, two of which were being raised by the crowd about to rush the gates.

Loftus, just behind them, led his party on their heels. He saw one of the men with a gun raise it, then bring it heavily down on a policeman's head, the ranks of the cordon broke; it could not resist that avalanche of crazed human beings.

Loftus fought his way to the man with the gun, then brought out his automatic. He clubbed good and hard. He heard the man gasp, saw him fall. He wrenched the rifle from his hand, then cleared a wider space about him with it. He saw men struggling back towards the gates—but in that brief moment of respite the cordon had regained its control. It reformed, strengthened by the Errols, Davidson, Best, Dunster and Grey.

The roaring grew deafening.

But through it filtered another sound, and suddenly there was a shrieking from the crowd. The deep growl of heavy vehicles followed, and Loftus saw at the far end of the Mall, a little column of armoured cars approaching very slowly.

There was no shooting; no bare steel.

The fight near the Embassy was getting more violent, yet he knew that it was the last effort, the final spurt of the dying candle of revolt. Against the threat of armoured cars the crowd must clear quickly.

He reached the steps of the building, saw men running. The crowd began to fall back, screaming, forgetful of its first purpose.

Loftus, rifle under his arm and breathing heavily, gasped:

'Some got through, you said?'

'Yes.'

'We'll make it inside,' said Loftus. 'It's all right out here now.'

He did not feel any particular relief at that, for he was afraid of what the mob would do inside the Embassy. He went through, seeing three or four little groups of scuffling people. Department men were busy, and he heard snapped orders from a police inspector in uniform. He saw a group of uniformed men come towards him and his party, and he shouted:

'Loftus—Loftus!'

Then from the stairs, where two groups were fighting desperately, came a stentorian shout:

'Let them through!'

Loftus looked up to see a big, burly man, flushed with the heat of the fight. This was Superintendent Miller, liaison officer between the Yard and the Department. Miller's sandy hair was dishevelled and he had lost his hat, but he obviously believed that he was on top of the situation.

Loftus reached him.

'Hoppermann?' he said.

'In the basement.'

'We'd better get there,' said Loftus.

He had to shout to make his voice heard even three yards away from him. His party turned, fighting their way towards the bottom of the staircase and then along the passage running by it. Miller followed them, with Loftus. He shouted directions, and they passed through the domestic quarters of the Embassy. There were more soldiers; clearly the military had concentrated on getting the inside of the Embassy safe. There were men lying in odd positions, across tables, on chairs, on the floor. There were occasional *mêlées*, but for the most part the rooms near the entrance to the basement were clear.

Miller said, heavily:

'It's the old air-raid shelter, where most of the records are kept. I got Hoppermann down there as soon as possible.'

Soon they reached the entrance to the basement, and a policeman in uniform saluted.

'All clear here, sir.'

'Good,' said Miller. 'We'll go down.'

The staircase was lighted by electricity. Two or three soldiers lined it, with fixed bayonets. As they neared the basement itself, a stronger party of soldiers stopped them, and Miller had some difficulty in getting past. But the door leading to the main shelter was opened at last, and Loftus and his men stepped through.

The atmosphere was cool and calm. The closed door kept out most of the sound from above, and little groups of men were standing and chatting. Loftus, looking about him, saw Hoppermann talking to a tall, grey-haired man, very familiar to most people because of the frequency with which his photographs appeared in the Press. It was Stillson, the United States Ambassador.

By them was the stocky Goss.

It was the first time Loftus had seen him since the affair at the Strand office when he had first learned that Hoppermann was alive, and he eyed the bodyguard curiously. Goss had a hand in his pocket; there was little doubt that he carried a gun. He glared at Loftus and the others suspiciously, and muttered something under his breath.

Hoppermann looked up.

He smiled suddenly when he saw and recognised Loftus, and Loftus was aware of a quick admiration for a man who behaved so coolly and naturally, although the mob outside had been crying for his blood.

'Well, Loftus,' he drawled. 'On the job again, I see. I was just talking of you.' He turned to Stillson, and said easily: 'This is Loftus, who warned me it wasn't safe for me to go about.'

Stillson said gravely:

'I have heard of you, Mr. Loftus. You were very right.'

Loftus said: 'I hope this will be the end of it, sir.'

'The guy's kiddin',' said Goss sharply, from Hoppermann's side. 'It's all a put-up job, I tell you.'

Stillson eyed the bodyguard coldly. Loftus shrugged.

'You stick to your ideas, Goss, don't you?'

'They're the right ones,' snapped Goss.

Hoppermann put a hand on the man's shoulder.

'That's quite enough, Goss. I've explained him to you both, I think.'

'Yes,' said Loftus, still looking at Goss. 'Oh, well.' He paused, then turned towards Hoppermann. 'I know how this was arranged, and I can get in touch with most of the agitators. When that's done, I think we will have a story which will calm down public opinion in the States, gentlemen.'

'I hope that is true, Mr. Loftus,' said Stillson.

'It's going to look bad,' said Hoppermann. 'I won't forgive myself easily for this, Loftus. Since I've talked to Stillson and some of the others, I know it's wholly right that we should support you and N.A.T.O. I won't need that tour after all,' he added with a faint smile. 'But this *is* bad, I guess.'

'The effect at home can't be exaggerated,' said Stillson. 'I've tried, since I came here, to bring about a closer co-operation of the two countries, but—'

He paused, as if overcome by bitterness.

Hoppermann said: 'If I hadn't come—'

Stillson waved a hand. He was tall and pale-faced, spoke with a soft voice which had a persuasive attractiveness.

'It was as well, in some ways, you brought it to a head.'

Loftus turned to Hoppermann. 'They were stirred up to this, I think, and, as I've said, I know the man who's done the stirring. Once we've got him we'll be able to straighten things out.'

'I surely hope you're right,' said Hoppermann.

Someone called Stillson aside, and Hoppermann and Loftus stood for a moment without speaking.

Then Hoppermann began to talk, desultorily; and after a

little more than half-an-hour Miller, who had gone out, returned. He was smiling a little as he approached Stillson, who had rejoined Hoppermann and Loftus.

'It's all clear, sir. There'll be no more trouble.'

Stillson looked relieved. 'That's fine. You lost no time when you did get working.'

'We did our best, sir.'

Hoppermann lit a cigarette.

'Well, that's the end of it,' he said. 'Am I still confined to barracks, Loftus?'

'I don't think so,' said Loftus slowly. 'They've shot their bolt with this. Even if they kill you,' he added slowly, 'the effect couldn't be much worse.'

Hoppermann frowned. 'That's not saying much for me. Loftus, you've never believed that I meant what I said, have you? You've never thought me wholly sincere?'

Loftus smiled a little, not with humour.

'I wouldn't say that. I've been out of sympathy with you, but no more than that. Are you leaving the Embassy?'

'I'll go to my hotel,' said Hoppermann sharply. 'God damn it, Loftus, I won't be forced to hide any longer. *I've* brought this about. You think it, Stillson thinks it, everyone in authority is of the same opinion. All right, then, I'll face what's coming. I wanted to help my country, I had no other thought in mind. Twice before we helped England, and were robbed because of it. I came to try to make sure this was one time when America wasn't fooled. Well, I'll go out and make sure.'

He pushed his way towards the door leading to the stairs. Goss went with him, casting a single vicious glance at Loftus.

Mike Errol said: 'He's taken that badly, Bill.'

'You meant him to, didn't you?' asked Mark.

'Don't be an idiot,' said Loftus. 'Why should I? All right, we'll get after him. There's one thing we mustn't forget,' he added. 'We haven't got Lewis. And by following Hoppermann, we might get him. We'll have four men after him all the time, two concentrating on Hoppermann, two on Goss. Errols, Dunster and Grey, you can make a start. 'Phone the flat when you can, and I'll have you relieved. I'm going to see Craigie.'

Of the gravity of the effect of the riot on the American people there had been no doubt, but as the hours passed, while Hoppermann and Goss went on their fact-finding mission, always closely followed, reports came in by radio and cable, and it grew clear that a large section of the American Press was swinging over to the Isolationist viewpoint.

Arrests of 'A' subscribers to the *Journal* up and down the country went on unceasingly, but there was no trace of Lewis, and they had to get Lewis before the propaganda could be defeated. Each hour was vital, and each hour dragged; for Christine Weston as well as for Loftus and Oundle.

Finally it was an ordinary messenger boy, early on the Sunday morning, who brought a message; not to Loftus but to Christine. It said:

'Your father has been seriously injured. If you wish to see him again, I advise you to come at once to the Western Hotel, Southampton. Goss.'

21

HOW LONG TO LIVE

The messenger boy was standing outside, whistling under his breath. Christine stood reading the message for a second time, and Loftus and Oundle read it over her shoulder. In the following silence Loftus turned and strode to the open front door.

His voice sounded abruptly.

'How did you get this?'

'Office give it to me,' said the boy promptly.

Loftus tightened his lips.

'How long are they open on Sunday mornings?'

For the first time the messenger boy wilted, shuffling his feet.

'Only fer 'arf an hour, it ain't no use 'phoning them now, they're closed. You ought ter be grateful for me coming on a Sunday morning, that's what.'

'I ought to tan your hide,' said Loftus sharply. 'You had this late yesterday afternoon, didn't you?'

Any embryo hope of lying effectively clearly disappeared from the boy's mind. He admitted that it was true, that he had been in a hurry to go to the pictures and had forgotten the last message. It had been telephoned, and he knew it was a long-distance one because he had heard the clerk behind the counter talking about it.

The advantage of using the Quick Service, thought Loftus as he dismissed the youngster and returned to the room, was that there was no way of checking up on the dispatch of the message; a telegram would have been easily traced.

'Is that true, Bill? Was it handed in yesterday?'

'I'm afraid so,' said Loftus. 'I'm going to 'phone Craigie, while you and Ned get ready for a journey.'

He picked up the telephone and dialled Craigie's number.

''Morning, Gordon. Where was Hoppermann last reported?'

'At Portsmouth, yesterday morning.'

'H'm. Who was with him?'

'Mike and Mark, Dunster and Grey.'

Loftus didn't answer directly, and Craigie wondered what was on his mind. Suddenly Loftus spoke.

'We've had a message, supposedly from Goss, that Hoppermann's badly injured at the Western Hotel, Southampton. I'd say the message was sent at about five-thirty yesterday afternoon.'

Craigie's voice sharpened.

'I've heard nothing.'

'The Errols and the others would have been in touch if there'd been any trouble,' said Loftus. 'Any outward trouble, that is. But it's odd they haven't reported since yesterday morning. Will you try to get them at the Western? I'm driving down straight away, with Ned and Christine, and I'll 'phone again *en route*. But in case of accidents we'd better have some more of the lads down there.'

'I'll look after it, Bill. Go easy.'

Loftus replaced the receiver, and turning, found that Christine and Oundle were ready and waiting.

They talked little in the early stages of the journey.

At Virginia Water they stopped and, from the hotel, Loftus telephoned Craigie again. He was not surprised when Craigie confirmed that Goss and Hoppermann were at the Western Hotel, and had reached there the previous evening. The Errols, Dunster and Grey were also at the hotel, but had nothing out of the ordinary to report.

'Oh, well,' said Loftus. 'We'll see what it's all about in a few hours.'

He rang off, climbed back into the car, and passed on the information. Christine said slowly:

'So the message *was* sent to trap you.'

'It looks that way,' said Loftus.

'Do you think it was Goss who sent the message?'

Loftus pursed his lips.

'Not necessarily. He struck me as being an objectionable little bounder, but as loyal as they're made. I think he means what he says most of the time. But Lewis knows that he's working for your father, and would use his name in the message all right.'

'But how do you know that Lewis is at the back of this?' she demanded. 'How do you know he doesn't think he's done enough? He might have given the whole thing up.'

Loftus smiled.

'I don't know, I've just a feeling. But *someone* must have sent that message.' He leaned forward and spoke into Oundle's ear. 'If we have to imitate a snail, old man, make it a snail at running pace.'

Oundle grimaced, but the needle moved slowly upwards to the seventy mark on the straight stretches, and an hour later Oundle pulled the car up outside the Western Hotel.

'Get us some coffee, will you?' Loftus said to a waiter in the reception foyer; then looked up and saw Mike Errol.

Mike approached.

'Well, Bill? Craigie said you'd probably arrive.'

'And we have,' said Loftus unnecessarily. 'How are things?'

'Too damned quiet,' said Mike. 'Hoppermann hasn't stirred from his room, they're having all their meals sent in, and Goss only looks out occasionally.'

'Are they sharing the room?'

'They've a two-room suite with a bath.'

'H'm. It looks as if they came prepared for a long stay,' said Loftus. 'Nothing else at all?'

'Positively nothing at all,' said Mike. 'It's too darned quite altogether.'

'Have you seen Hoppermann since he came here?'

'No, not once.'

'He was all right when he arrived?'

'We-ell,' said Mike, glancing at Christine, who made a motion with her hand as if telling him to say exactly what he thought. 'He looked a bit pale and washed out, but he was walking on his own two legs, and didn't need Goss's support. They've had a pretty good run around since Friday morning. I'd like to know where they haven't been in the south and southwest,' he added.

'No attempt to molest them?'

'None at all.'

Loftus shrugged. 'Well, we'll see what there is to see in a few minutes.'

It had seemed a long drive, and they were glad of the coffee, which was brought quickly. It was nearly half-past twelve, and they ordered lunch for one-thirty. Dunster arrived downstairs just before they left the lounge; he had been watching the landing near Hoppermann's suite, but Grey had now taken over. Dunster looked tired, but was cheerful; there was nothing to report, he said.

Then he spoke more grimly.

'There's going to be real trouble with the States, Bill. The Sunday papers have made the splash of the year about that riot at the American Embassy.'

'Yes, there'll be trouble all right if we don't do something. Come on, Christine, we'll go up. Mike, stay outside Hoppermann's window. Dunster, watch this door. Ned, the back door.' He spoke crisply, resting a hand on Christine's elbow. 'We'll go up,' he repeated, 'and see how things are.'

'He can't be hurt,' said Christine helplessly. 'Ought you to go there? Aren't you afraid that someone will be waiting for you in the passage or one of the other rooms?'

'It could be,' said Loftus, 'but I don't think so.'

He knew the number of Hoppermann's suite from Mike Errol, and when they reached it he whispered to Christine to tap. She did so, and after a pause there came Goss's nasal voice:

'Who's there?'

'Mrs. Weston,' called Christine clearly.

'Stay put,' said Goss, and they heard the door being unlocked. It opened a fraction of an inch, and Goss held a hand to his coat pocket, doubtless about a gun. Christine stepped forward, and Loftus pushed the door open. Goss swore, but he did not use the gun which he snatched from his pocket.

He closed the door behind them, and locked it.

'I figured you'd come,' he said tartly. 'Keep it quiet, he's in a bad way.' He led the way to a door communicating with the second room of the suite, and as he opened it slowly Loftus and Christine looked through.

They saw the bed, facing the door, and the figure lying in

it. His face was recognisable, although his head was swathed in bandages. He was very pale, and his eyes were closed.

Loftus said: 'Goss, you've made a mistake.'

There was suddenly tension in the room, and Goss stepped back a pace. The two men stood by the open door, with the man on the bed in sight but, it seemed, not seeing them. Christine stood just inside the second room, wide-eyed.

'You and Hoppermann have been followed since you left the Embassy,' Loftus went on slowly. 'Nothing happened to Hoppermann *outside*. Only *you* could have injured him.'

Goss paled. His hands were a little unsteady, but he was wise enough not to raise his gun.

'It's a lie! He was shot through the window, the night we reached this dump!' he snarled. 'I didn't make a row, I didn't tell anyone, I wanted to give him a break. I'm a doctor, see, I'm qualified, I took care of him.'

Suddenly there was a shout from outside the window, and Loftus recognised Mike's voice, high-pitched in warning.

'Look out, Bill, look out!'

Loftus swung round, sweeping Christine to one side with his left arm. She lost her balance as he meant she should. Goss went flat on his stomach, while something crashed through the glass of the window, a small, round object which hit the foot of the bed.

The patient did not stir.

Loftus moved again. He saw the vague shape of a man outside the window, a man standing on a balcony. He thought it was Lewis, but he could not be sure. He reached the round object, picked it up, and carried it to the window.

It *was* Lewis!

He was on the balcony which connected the room they were in with the room next door, and he held a gun in his hand. It was the 'first' Lewis, tall, good-looking, but with his lips twisted and his eyes vicious in their hatred.

Loftus shouted: 'Get clear, Mike!'

As he did so he swung open the glass door opening on to the balcony, stepped outside, and tossed the round object towards Lewis.

He heard the man take in a deep breath, then, as he backed away, Loftus *saw* the explosion. He had no time to get at a safe distance. The flame, the blast, followed in quick succession. Loftus was thrown against the side of the balcony. He felt a dreadful pain in his legs, and when he tried to get to his feet he could not do so. He heard shouting, but it was vague and confused.

He was lying on his side.

He saw Christine come from the room, and step towards him. Behind her was Goss. He saw Mike Errol appear, suddenly; Mike had come up by a fire escape, and was climbing over the balcony. He said in a low voice:

'Watch all doors, Mike, make sure we get him.'

Then he tightened his lips against the pain.

22

GO AWAY DEATH

C hristine was conscious only of the fact that Loftus was lying hurt. She saw that he was conscious, saw him close his eyes suddenly, and clench his teeth. She swung round on Goss.

'If you're a doctor, *do* something!'

But Goss was staring at Lewis.

There was no chance at all that he would live; there was little that he was still alive. Goss's lips were working; but he swung round on Mike Errol, and raised his gun.

He began to swear.

Errol, also armed, fired without wasting time and Goss's gun went flying from his grasp. He stooped to get the gun, but Mike reached across and clubbed him. Goss gasped, then went down, quite unconscious.

Mike stepped through the casement windows.

On the bed was the bandaged figure, the eyes closed. There was no indication that Hoppermann had been disturbed, although there was broken glass scattered across the room, pictures had been thrown from the walls, everything which had been on the dressing-table, chest and mantelpiece, was now lying smashed on the floor. But Hoppermann remained quite still.

Mike muttered: 'Is—is he dead?'

Then he heard almost the last thing he expected, or it was Loftus's voice, from the balcony.

'Mike—Mike—'

Christine appeared, then came a heavy knocking on the door. Mike ignored it, and ran back to the balcony.

'Hurry,' said Christine urgently.

Loftus, sweating from the pain, looked up into Errol's eyes, and muttered:

'The thing—on the bed—a dummy. *Hoppermann's—about —somewhere. Get him. Try—next door—Lewis's room.'*

Mike Errol waited just long enough to take the words in. He saw Christine opening the door, to Grey, Mark and Martin Best—Martin had arrived, it transpired, a few minutes before.

'Hoppermann's about, get him!' he snapped.

He went along to the piece of masonry across the balcony which separated Lewis's room from Hoppermann's, climbed the balcony, and reached the next window. He saw a man sitting in front of a dressing-table, doing something to his hair; a dark-haired man. He put an elbow to the window, and cracked in the glass.

The man at the dressing-table spun round.

There was a gun near his hand, and he snatched at it, but Mike Errol was ready for that and fired from the hip. He struck the other's gun, sending it spinning out of the man's hand. He went through after breaking the window open. The man had grabbed at a chair with his left hand, raised it, and flung it at Mike. It missed by inches. Mike fired again, saw the man clutch at his right forearm.

He said in a low-pitched voice:

'Keep right there, or you'll get one lower down.' He raised his voice: 'Grey—this room. *Grey!*' The sound died away, but in a few seconds Grey, Best and Mark were crowding into the room, where the man still stood by the dressing-table. His dark hair was a little on one side; he was a big man, Mike saw.

Mike stepped across and pulled at the dark hair; he was not surprised that it came off, and he saw the iron-grey hair of Cyrus K. Hoppermann. The eyes, too, were unmistakable, and when the grease-paint was washed from his face Mike knew that he would show a healthy freshness of complexion. Mike had expected it from the moment Loftus had spoken, yet it was still a shock, an almost unbelievable thing.

Hoppermann, here. Hoppermann, affecting a disguise to try to get away. Hoppermann, in Lewis's room.

Mike said sharply: 'Get an ambulance, and hurry. Bill's on the balcony. I hope to God—'

His voice tailed off, and in that moment each Department man forgot Hoppermann, and thought only of Bill Loftus. In that moment, too, Hoppermann seemed to realise it, for he made a move towards the door. But he reckoned without Best, who hit him, sending him reeling against the wall. He did not try to move again.

It was one hour before they had finished searching, but they found nothing of great importance. Hoppermann had been taken to the local police station, Loftus to the nearest hospital.

Christine had gone with Loftus; now she was waiting while they operated, and going over what Loftus had said in the ambulance. In a peculiarly automatic way she made notes of it; his words seemed to be burned into her mind.

'I thought it was your father, Christine. Sorry. I think there were two motives. Hatred—of England, And greed.'

'How, Bill?' she had asked.

'He had control of Nu-Steel, and he wanted control of the other firms, Atlantic Coast Shipping, Radio—he wanted them all. He started this terror-campaign in America against the other magnates, although serving on their Committee and organising them *against* co-operation. He put the terror-campaign down to English agents, worked up feeling against Britain, and all the time he schemed to get control of their companies.'

'I—see.'

'He tried to buy up all possible Nu-Steel shares, too. *He wanted absolute control of all the companies which were engaged in armaments, or dependent industries.* It was—' Loftus paused, and drew a deep breath, then went on '—a grandiose scheme. Complete control. He's rich, he could afford to buy a lot, he could squeeze shares out of the companies whose directors were frightened for their lives. More steel—more goods—more of everything. His profits would pile up, every extra day of international tension meant extra profits. And he saw himself as industrial dictator of America, I think. I can't see—any other—solution.'

Christine said: 'He—had dreamed of it.'

'You knew that?'

'I thought it was just talk. I couldn't conceive of *this*.'

The ambulance had reached the hospital, and Loftus had been carried on a stretcher to the operating room, but he talked all the way to those doors quickly, feverishly, and she knew that he was talking thus because he thought he was going to die, and wanted to make sure that someone knew exactly what was in his mind.

'It's—bad. But—I must finish. It wasn't altogether—succeeding. He decided—to come here. Ostensibly, to see for himself. Actually, to make arrangements. He sent a stooge, who was killed in the airways-crash. He knew it would happen, *he planned it to make it look like an attack on him.* He arranged the same thing at the office. Guggleheim tried to tell me that he hadn't gone to kill Hoppermann officially, that actually he was to make a show and then get away, *but Guggleheim happened to be a genuine anti-American, so he tried to do the job properly.'*

'Yes,' said Christine.

'We shall be ready in five minutes,' said a nurse.

'I must finish,' said Loftus urgently. 'Everything was planned to make it look as if the Lewis organisation was aiming to get Hoppermann—it was a perfect cover. Hoppermann gave Sell the buying orders through Lewis, Sell thought he was working against his employer, and that caused quarrels. Lewis was here, with the organisation ready and the big bluff also set—the Manfrey-Pellisser-Gott bluff, intended to get us thinking one way while they worked in another. *Leathercraft* enabled Lewis to keep in touch with his agents, as well as a host of fools who think that England to-day can stand alone as she did a hundred years ago. The Embassy riot was to put the Hoppermann angle well over and to cause the trouble in the States; and by God it succeeded! But I'd let Hoppermann know, or guess, that I suspected him. I let him think that, when I talked to him at the Embassy. I knew we couldn't get him unless he showed his hand.'

'Which he did, aiming to get me there by sending for you, I saw that thing on the bed was a dummy, there was no sign of breathing, and the face was too waxy white even for a dead man. In any case, Goss was too devoted to him to act as he did if he was in real danger.'

'I believed they would try to kill me. The most obvious thing seemed that Lewis was already at the hotel, that he would act and Hoppermann would contrive to get away after pretending to be injured. He could have gone into a nursing-home, or what was supposed to be one, and "recover" at leisure. Lewis, who worked for him, had one job left—to kill me. It worked much as I expected. The final scene, throwing a bomb into the room where Hoppermann was supposed to be, was intended to kill two birds with one stone—put Hoppermann in the clear *and* finish me off. It was a delayed action bomb to give Goss, who knew it was coming and what it was, time to take cover. I, not expecting it, would have been killed, Goss would have hidden the dummy, and Hoppermann would have nipped back into bed. They didn't think—I'd throw it back at—Lewis.'

The nurse reappeared. 'We're ready now, I'll just—'

'A moment,' interrupted Loftus sharply. 'Christine, outline all that to Craigie. Your father must be made to confess, somehow. Tell the other fellows, and—'

He paused, his face twisted in a spasm of pain. Then he said slowly:

'Tell them, thanks. It's been a good run. Odd, so soon after Diana—'

'Bill,' said Christine slowly, 'don't give up. No matter what happens, don't give up. Diana wouldn't want it; I didn't know her but I'm sure she wouldn't. Hold on, Bill.'

He looked at her, wonderingly.

'It's not—up to me. Oh, Christine—you broke with your father because you married an Englishman. My first clue. He hated Englishmen, and his daughter married one. And he fell into a simple trick, by getting into a waiting cab. Goss as a bodyguard, would have taught him better than that. And— Hoppermann was allowed to escape at Putney to—to "prove" he wasn't implicated. One other thing: You. You could have told of his hatred of England, you were dangerous beyond all people. And—you helped me, all along. You started me on the right angle, and I stuck to it. I—thanks, Christine.'

'I'm sorry,' said the nurse, 'we really must get the patient ready.'

What spirit there had been in Hoppermann was crushed by the fight at Southampton, and within twenty-four hours he had made a full confession. He confirmed Loftus's theories, and elaborated them. For years he had been getting control of the big corporations and he had most of them in his hands. As Loftus had surmised, by inspiring anti-British feeling in America, he both increased his profits, and at the same time, worked off an inborn hatred of all things British.

He had not been in touch with any foreign agents.

The German papers were planted at *Conway* to create that impression, and Lewis had always tried to do the same—but he was answerable only to Hoppermann.

Goss was in it, of course; Goss, who also hated all things British.

Loftus was out of the operating room after two hours, but had not come round. The same message was received hour after hour.

Christine, in constant touch with the hospital, was white-faced, hard-eyed. Oundle talked very little, for it seemed there was nothing to say.

And then, after thirty-six hours, a message: *'The patient has recovered consciousness.'* Christine took it, on the phone, and turned to Oundle, her eyes suddenly bright and moist.

'He's come round. There's a chance.'

Oundle said: 'If he's conscious and wants to come out, he'll make it. He *must* make it, Christine, we can't do without him. But—' he too looked pale. 'What he'll do when he knows, that's beyond me. Bill forced to keep sitting down; Bill, when he knows he's had a leg amputated—'

'Stop it!' snapped Christine tensely. 'Stop it!'

In another six hours there was a message from the hospital; Loftus could see Mrs. Weston and Mr. Oundle for a few minutes. He was weak, but stronger than he had been, although of course, he must not be excited.

They hurried there, and were taken to the small private ward. Loftus was lying on the bed, with one leg, his only leg, strapped up and slung above body-level, so that the blood should not run into it. His face was almost as pale as the sheets, but his eyes were open. He turned his head slowly, and a faint smile curved his lips.

Close to the bed, they heard:

'Hallo, you two. How's tricks?'

Oundle said: 'Everything's all right, Bill. America, I mean.'

'Of course, it is. Sound people, Americans, when they know the truth. Anyone else hurt?'

'No.'

'We were lucky.' He was quiet for a moment, then he went on: 'Well, it's a fine do. Better order me a very good new leg.'

Christine exclaimed: 'You know about it?'

'Oh, yes. Too bad. But I'll hold on, and Craigie'll find me something to do somewhere. Tell—tell young Mayo I'll be seeing him. Er—Christine.'

'Yes, Bill.'

'You were quite right. Women often are, bless 'em. It'll be worth it.' He smiled again, and then a nurse came in and ushered them away; but they were no longer afraid.

A man in a bath-chair and a young boy with ginger hair were together on the courtyard of Buckingham Palace, on a day when the King was decorating many men and women for bravery. It had taken Hershall a long time to persuade Loftus to accept the decoration, which was the highest 'civilian' honour; Jimmy Mayo, also to be decorated, probably weighed the scales.

Ned Oundle pushed the chair, and Christine, the Errols,

Best, Dunster, Grey, and a dozen others, were outside, watching the ceremony.

Christine saw Loftus smile, and talk for a few moments with a gracious sovereign, saw Jimmy Mayo salute stiffly, saw Oundle begin to push the chair away. Christine forced her way to the gates, and reached them as the chair came out. Loftus was looking about the crowd, saw her, and smiled widely. The sun glinted on the medal on his chest.

'Wasn't it *won*-derful!' exclaimed Jimmy, low-voiced. 'Isn't *he* grand?'

Christine said: 'Yes, isn't he?' and looked at Loftus.

ABOUT THE AUTHOR

John Creasey, born in 1908, was a paramount English crime and science fiction writer who used myriad pseudonyms for more than six hundred novels. He founded the UK Crime Writers' Association in 1953. In 1962, his book *Gideon's Fire* received the Edgar Award for Best Novel from the Mystery Writers of America. Many of the characters featured in Creasey's titles became popular, including George Gideon of Scotland Yard, who was the basis for a subsequent television series and film. Creasey died in Salisbury, UK, in 1973.

DEPARTMENT Z

FROM OPEN ROAD MEDIA

OPEN ROAD

INTEGRATED MEDIA

OPEN ROAD

INTEGRATED MEDIA

Find a full list of our authors and
titles at www.openroadmedia.com

FOLLOW US
@OpenRoadMedia